THE LYON WHO LOVED ME

The Lyon's Den Connected World

Tracy Sumner

Dragonblade Publishing, Inc. is an imprint of Kathryn Le Veque Novels, Inc.
P.O. Box 23
Moreno Valley, CA 92556
ceo@dragonbladepublishing.com

Produced in the United States of America

First Edition September 2023
Print Edition

ARE YOU SIGNED UP FOR DRAGONBLADE'S BLOG?

You'll get the latest news and information on exclusive giveaways, exclusive excerpts, coming releases, sales, free books, cover reveals and more.

Check out our complete list of authors, too!

No spam, no junk. That's a promise!

Sign Up Here

www.dragonbladepublishing.com

Dearest Reader;

Thank you for your support of a small press. At Dragonblade Publishing, we strive to bring you the highest quality Historical Romance from some of the best authors in the business. Without your support, there is no 'us', so we sincerely hope you adore these stories and find some new favorite authors along the way.

Happy Reading!

CEO, Dragonblade Publishing

Other Lyon's Den Books

Into the Lyon of Fire by Abigail Bridges
Lyon of the Highlands by Emily Royal
The Lyon's Puzzle by Sandra Sookoo
Lyon at the Altar by Lily Harlem
Captivated by the Lyon by C.H. Admirand
The Lyon's Secret by Laura Trentham
The Talons of a Lyon by Jude Knight
The Lyon and the Lamb by Elizabeth Keysian
To Claim a Lyon's Heart by Sherry Ewing
A Lyon of Her Own by Anna St. Claire
Don't Wake a Sleeping Lyon by Sara Adrien
The Lyon and the Bluestocking by E.L. Johnson
The Lyon's Perfect Mate by Cerise DeLand

At the touch of love, everyone becomes a poet.

~Plato

PROLOGUE

Where an engagement is soundly broken

A deserted chapel
Richmond, England 1816

H E WASN'T GOING to show.

Wilhelmina Wright released a defeated sigh and sank to the marble steps leading to a medieval altar that would host no celebration this day. She ripped the veil from her face and let it flutter like a flag of surrender to the ancient flagstones. Taking a breath crawling with the scent of freesia from her bridal posy, she concluded that Griffin Alistair Beckett, fourth or fifth or seventieth Viscount Kent, was indeed a rat bastard.

Much as he was rumored to be.

She should have known better than to trust anyone in the aristocracy—blue blood and lies, the lot of them. And debt, enough liability to force loveless arrangements such as these through the marital channels every day. She huffed and yanked her chignon free, hoping to ease the headache plaguing her. Her flaxen hair tumbled past her shoulders, the only bit of life she'd yet to overpower.

Oh, and a viscount who'd thought to leave her sitting on her bum in a chapel in the middle of nowhere.

She'd assumed her intended was arrogant, of course. A man who closely resembled a Greek god couldn't be anything but conceited. He likely imagined he was also the most intelligent bloke in the room, certainly cleverer than a mere female. This deficit she could have managed, not because it was true, but because it was what they all believed. However, Lord Kent had seemed, during their brief introduction two weeks ago, to be honorable or wishing to *be* honorable, his days of White's betting book wagers and wild carriage races down Bond over. The actresses, opera singers, and jaded wives no longer his to pursue. No more duels or climbing from second-story windows to escape enraged husbands.

According to him, he was cleaning up his life.

Mina dragged her slipper through the multicolored stripe thrown from the stained glass above her head and compiled a list of benefits of leaving this chapel unwed. She wasn't a chit to cry over blunders in planning.

For one, it would have been extremely hard to pledge to obey. She didn't believe in submitting without negotiation. Blind adherence was not something she was comfortable with. Two, she wasn't sure about this sexual congress business. She'd heard contrasting reviews in whispered parlors, most of them ominous. She chewed on her thumbnail as a dangerous sizzle rippled through her belly.

Although the reviews about Viscount Kent—and after meeting him, she trusted them—were impressive.

She had high ideals even as she'd planned to sell herself short. Her parents' marriage had been an excellent partnership, equals bound by love until they were forever parted after cholera swept their borough when Mina was nine. Then, it had been left to her father to parent his only child as best he could. Andrew Wright, the owner of a racecourse that rivaled Epsom but was fashioned for the lower classes, had supported education for his daughter, providing tutors and books rather than his attention or love. From a distance, he'd encouraged her to voice her views without mentioning that the world outside Wright's Grand Derby wouldn't appreciate her candor.

He'd died two years ago, leaving her with bold opinions, an inheritance large enough to kill a moose, and a pervading loneliness he'd not sought to ease in his lifetime.

Mina dropped her chin to her fist. Perhaps Griffin Beckett had heard about her willfulness, or God forbid, her secret endeavor, which had nothing to do with horses. All she'd wanted was a title to hide behind, a man who wished to manage her father's business—and possibly, someday, give her children. A lady of standing, a viscountess, could champion any cause she desired, including running a discreet enterprise. She lost the occasional client when they realized an unmarried woman operated W.L.W. Investigations, although the dubious nature of her commissions kept her clients from being overly choosy. A proper union would have calmed the few who cared.

Lord Kent needed blunt to save his estates, a tired but true story when she'd more than enough to share. It could have been the perfect solution if the groom had opted to attend his wedding.

For Mina, money wasn't the problem. *Freedom* was.

Temper brewing, she plucked at her skirt, a satiny champagne rose that had made a reasonably lovely wedding gown, then stomped her foot on the flagstones, sending a swirl of dust rising around her. There was no concern about anyone witnessing this disaster as she had no family left, and the bridegroom had chosen not to invite his, so she was alone, except for her erstwhile matchmaker and the vicar snoring in the last pew.

Mina glanced around, her sigh echoing off the stone. It was an adorable spot should this have been where her life took another direction.

Damn him. Now, she'd have to go back to the drawing board.

As if she heard the whispered oath, Mrs. Bessie Dove-Lyon, the Black Widow of Whitehall, slipped into the chapel through the arched side door, the veil covering her face fluttering in the breeze. Before the scrap of lace fluttered back into place, Mina caught sight of a stubbornly rounded chin that equaled her matchmaker's trenchant demeanor.

Surprising her, the Black Widow settled beside Mina on the top step, a hesitant but determined show of support. "This was a gamble, my dear. A failed one, it appears." She rolled her shoulders with a pained murmur. "I'm not sure how to take it. My agreements are rarely breached, my strategies rarely disputed."

Mina reached for her cloak, searching a pocket and coming out with a dented silver carafe bearing the initials *A.C.W.* She'd packed her father's flask in the event she needed liquid mettle for her wedding night. She offered it to Mrs. Dove-Lyon, who shook her head, her censorious hum rattling her veil.

"Agreeing to anything with Lord Kent was a gamble," Mina said against the decanter's grooved rim. "I should have realized what a risk it was accepting the man."

The Black Widow laughed softly. "I meant you, Miss Wright. *You* are the gamble. I thought the other piece of this puzzle was confirmed. I expected him to show up, the gutless knave. My dear Colonel would be supremely disappointed."

Mina coughed, brandy leaving a fiery trail in its wake. She wasn't much of a drinker, but now seemed a good time to start. "*I'm* the gamble?" And what did Mrs. Dove-Lyon's late husband have to do with this?

Her matchmaker patted her hand, only part of the gesture patronizing. "Your father was a dear friend. He helped me when finances were tight during the opening of the Lyon's Den. When I could not find men willing to make repairs and provide security, as I was such an uncertain wager myself. I never forgot his kindness or his understanding of the plight I was facing. Or his beautiful, bright hooligan of a daughter. When you came to me for assistance locating a husband, I thought, 'Wilhelmina Wright is not suited for just any man.' There's something exceptional about you, my dear."

Mina glanced down in embarrassment, rarely on the receiving end of compliments.

The Black Widow clicked her tongue against her teeth. "I needed a desperate gentleman, true, of which there are scores in London, but also one who would be tolerant when he found himself attached to a headstrong wife. A more accommodating sort than is typical in society. A man with a heart, even if the heart is buried deep. I believed I had located him in Viscount Kent."

Mina would have refuted the unflattering statement—but a desperate husband is what she'd needed. Due to the missing groom, *still* needed. "Regrettably, my reputation may have presented more of a challenge than your 'accommodating sort' could take."

"My dear," Mrs. Dove-Lyon whispered with what Mina assumed was a steady smile, "you're a lioness in satin. I wanted to find you a lion to match. I was aware of the challenges."

Mina twisted her fingers in her skirt. "If I ever get my hands on your lion, he'll be sorry." Although, she didn't mean it. Of course, when she realized he wasn't coming, she'd wanted her intended bruised and bloody.

Then she remembered the cats.

Griffin Beckett liked cats.

Something about this remained with her weeks after their first and only meeting. She'd had fur on her sleeve that morning in the Lyon's Den, for which she'd apologized profusely. She'd been tending a litter born in the stable the previous evening. Rather than frustration, his smile had been positively delightful as he listened to her stammering explanation. Then he'd mentioned a litter living in *his* stable in Hertfordshire, three males and a mama, all a blazing tabby orange.

She'd have enjoyed having a husband who loved animals.

Mina tapped the flask against her teeth. Lastly, her little secret…

He'd called her Willie.

Turning away from the Black Widow, Mina pressed a smile into her fist. *Willie.* It was ridiculous, and sadly, she'd been utterly charmed. Aside from her father's employees, no one had flirted, teased, or even talked to her. Men seemed repelled by her impudence or disgusted by her lowly station. Her sturdy attractiveness, confirmed in her mirror, hadn't been enough to overcome the burden.

Whatever it was, the opposite sex stayed away as if a foul aroma were attached.

Consequently, she hadn't known what to do with Lord Kent's playfulness, like Mrs. Dove-Lyon didn't know what to do with a collapse in planning.

They were both baffled by the situation. And the man.

Decidedly, she leaned in to catch Mrs. Dove-Lyon's gaze through the lace wall. "Let Lord Kent go. I've heard rumors of punitive consequences should anyone cross you, and if he's in trouble due to breaking your contract, I'll double my fee to compensate for the disruption to your schedule. I want it over, done." She curled her fingers around the flask, hating to ask, but having to ask. "I would like to arrange for your services. Again. If you'll agree to work with me. My needs are, as yet, unmet."

A stab of disappointment pricked Mina's usually thick skin as Griffin Beckett's pleasing visage flashed through her mind. Amorous activities with such a handsome creature might have been enjoyable. Maybe. Possibly.

But in the end, what did having a gorgeous husband do for a woman? She shrugged. *Nothing.*

The Black Widow shoved to her feet and began pacing, feasibly energized at collecting double her fee and an additional payment for a new undertaking. "Baron Riley-Fitzgerald was one I considered for you, and I still have him on the hook. He's quite frantic to locate assets as his estate in Derbyshire is nearing insolvency. His clock is ticking."

Mina groaned and banged the flask against her knee. Riley-Fitzgerald's face was enough to curdle milk. And his constitution? Milquetoast. On the plus side, she wouldn't have to fend off society chits as she surely would have with Griffin Beckett. She'd have had to watch her back—and his broad, sculpted one—every second. "I suppose he could do," she replied, breathing through her nose. The piquant aroma of incense was making her queasy.

Or perhaps that was the thought of bedding the baron.

"Mayhap, we've learned our lesson, dear. Weaker men are easier to coerce." The Black Widow halted in place, her skirt swirling around her ankles. She pointed to Mina with a determined jab. "I won't be as honest about your obdurate tendencies this time."

Mina took a sip without comment, as it was a sound plan.

"Although I didn't detail the exact nature of your business as it's your concern, of course. But I don't want those types knocking on the Den's door, and it horrifies me they knock on yours. Whomever we secure, and we *will* secure someone, it shall be up to you to inform them about your activities. Don't despair, Miss Wright. I owe your father, and Bessie Dove-Lyon never leaves a debt unpaid."

And that, Mina supposed, with brandy warming her because no husband was going to, was that.

GRIFFIN ALISTAIR BECKETT, fifth Viscount Kent, was about to do something most men wouldn't.

He was skipping his wedding.

Griff wrenched against the rope binding him to the chair, unsurprised that the thugs who'd dragged him into a rented hack an hour ago had strung him up well enough to secure him for eternity.

Regrettably, they seemed experienced kidnappers.

"Can someone please give me the time?" he asked, searching the dank warehouse for a clock. The dwelling reeked of labor and various scents bound to the products amassed in stacks around him. Spices, lumber, blood oranges. He coughed into his sleeve, the aroma of citrus nearly overpowering. The last shot of sunlight flowed through a grimy pane high above his head, as were the shouts of dockhands inundating the public houses lining the street.

The day over, his wedding over.

If he survived this, Bessie Dove-Lyon was going to kill him. He'd never heard of a man escaping the Black Widow's tangled web.

Even if the gent was family of the distant and by-marriage variety.

"You have somewhere else to be, my lord Kent?" the hoodlum who'd introduced himself as Jimmie Beans mumbled, a crimson-tipped cheroot dangling from his lips.

Wincing, Griff dabbed at his bruised lip with his tongue. They'd not been considerate when they hustled him into the carriage, although he'd fought them when he shouldn't have. Four against one when the four had grown up in the rookery, and the one in Mayfair presented a grossly unfair fight. There was desperation, and then, there was *desperation*. Exhaling hard, he shoved aside his anger. His wits would get him out of this mess, not his fists. "I do. My wedding."

The cheroot bobbled in Jimmie's mouth. "Are you foolin'?"

Griff grimaced and rolled his aching shoulders. "I'm not, unfortunately." For a split second, he experienced something akin to grief. The martial arrangement he'd agreed to was as far from a love match as could be designed, but he'd not been dreading marrying Wilhelmina Wright, for reasons he couldn't outline. During their brief meeting at the Lyon's Den, he'd seen a genuine flash of spirit in her, unlike the chirping annoyances in the *ton*. Too, she'd been the most fetching woman he'd ever laid eyes on or close to it. Her hair alone, flaxen and as thick as the rope tangled about him, enough to make a man weep.

Who needed bloody love when your wife looked like a goddess?

"A ceremony makes sense." Jimmie bobbed his head, sucking air through a gap in his yellowing teeth. "Proper reason for posh attire. Seemed a step up from a lord's normal rig. Sorry we made a muck of your fine outfit."

A voice from the back said: "It's one of them Lyon's Den trades."

All gazes shifted to the youngest person in the space, a young man they'd called Streeter. He looked part something, Romani perhaps, his jet-black hair overlong and dusting a set of startlingly green eyes. The lad shrugged, years of unconcern likely beaten into him. "I have a friend who works security at the Lyon's Den. Talk is raging about the match between Viscount Kent and the lady owner of Wright's. He forced, she paying. The Black Widow's usual deal."

Jimmie yanked his cheroot from his mouth and roared with laughter, jabbing the smoking stub Griff's way. "She'll hook the chit you've just abandoned at the holy bench another fine fish next week. Dove-Lyon has a list as long as her arm of fancy nobs needing blunt, or so they say. As for you, we have an easier way to save what's yours than wedding some troublesome gel born at the racetrack. All nice and tidy, wrapped up like a present without getting yourself a countess you don't want."

"Viscountess," Griff whispered, again thinking of Wilhelmina Wright and how she—deep in her heart, not that hardened façade one had to fashion to survive—was going to handle his not showing for what should be the most important day of her life. He wanted to forget that brood of kittens she'd mentioned with such kindness lingering in her lavender eyes, but he hadn't been able to.

Jimmie snapped his fingers, regaining Griff's attention. "Listen up, mate. What I'm presenting means everyone will end up happy, everyone will end up *safe*. No need to bring a new wife into this unpleasantness your cursed brother done caused, anyway, am I right? I have two younger ones meself, neither worth a damn, truth of it. I'm saving them left and right. I feel for you, in part."

Griff let his breath settle. Unease was an emotion he didn't need to share with this interesting group. Just because he'd give his life for his siblings didn't mean he wanted to give his life for his siblings. "What did he do this time?"

Jimmie perched his hulking frame on a wine cask, his grin friendly enough to charm if one found murderous grins charming. "Your brother is the worst gambler I've ever seen. I kicked him out of my place in Seven Dials last month, but he somehow returned the next night and lost all he had and more. Only relation of a titled nob I've ever had at the Lucky Penny as we ain't Crockfords. Once got a baron who stumbled in, but he was looking for the opium palace on Monmouth."

Seven Dials. Christ. Griff scrubbed his shoulder over his mouth, this conversation more painful than his split lip. "This isn't news, Mr. Beans. I'm aware of Dominic's failings and his inability to read a room." His brother had brought the Becketts to the brink of insolvency, risking the estate in Hertfordshire *and* the townhouse in Hanover Square, properties Griff had sworn on his father's deathbed to protect for future generations. Saving a family from disgrace and financial ruin was the only dream for first-born sons these days.

Jimmie flicked ashes to the floor and stomped on them. "This is my offer, Kent. I want you to come work for me. For six months, then you and that hapless brother of yours are free. No one the wiser. You need blunt, and I need sweet talk in a stylish suit of clothes."

What the hell? Griff tried to repress the stunned amusement that left his nose in a snorting burst.

Jimmie shoved off the cask, yanking his braces and letting them pop against his chest. "I know your breed don't hustle, it's looked down on, but I need investors for an enterprise." He tapped his temple with another whistle through his teeth. "A good one. Potential for returns is guaranteed. I have the idea, now I need the polish. Might take some legislative support if you get my meaning, which your kind works in that House of theirs every blessed day."

"Nothing is guaranteed except death, Mr. Beans. I have no issue dirtying my hands in trade if that's what you're implying. How could I when I've been reduced to contracting with marriage brokers who are likely more threatening than you? But this"—he glanced around the dimly lit space, nodding to the chair he was bound to—"is not how I wish to enter into a business arrangement. Ever."

"Told you," Streeter murmured from a dark corner. "More finesse with nobs is required."

Jimmie kicked a scrap of rubbish aside, a scowl pulling his lips low. "Ain't Bessie Dove-Lyon's methods the same but without the rope?"

Griff laughed, unable to help himself. "Now that you mention it…"

"I'm talking legitimate commerce, Kent. Investors, contracts, the whole deal laid on the table for every git to see. I have solicitors, the same ones your lot uses." Jimmie tunneled his hand in his frayed coat pocket, withdrawing another cheroot and jamming it between his lips. "Well, it'd be *almost* legitimate."

"So, you're not intent on killing me, is that it?"

"We're businessmen, mate. Not executioners."

Griff didn't know if he believed that, but he wasn't at liberty to argue. "I don't work for anyone. But *with*, that's a distinct possibility. Depending upon the circumstances."

The hoodlum put flint to tinder, sending the aroma of sulfur drifting about the room. "Don't forget, the Becketts owe me and owe me big."

Griff exhaled through his teeth, picturing kicking Dominic's arse all over London. However, this was *his* failing: intrepid curiosity. When someone told Griffin Alistair Beckett not to do something, he was the first across the finish line. The spark of interest racing through his veins was dangerous, possibly deadly, he judged as he tossed another glance around the warehouse. He knew it, yet he'd never been able to command it, either.

The marriage he'd agreed to had felt like a gamble in the most thrilling of ways.

Griff made a show of his indecision and would have buffed his nails on his trousers if he could. "What vile deed do I have to accomplish to crawl out of my brother's pit?" Smiling, he went in for the kill. "Too, if I'm acquiring investors of the titled variety, shouldn't I be rewarded for my industry by becoming one myself? If the idea has merit."

Jimmie stilled, his cheeks flushing an eager, florid red. "Partners? Risky circumstance for a posh toff, innit?"

Griff yanked against his tether, his gaze narrowing. "If I'm going to sell a product or service, I'd damned well better know everything about it. I can't do that trussed up like a turkey set to bake."

Jimmie snapped his fingers, calling for whisky and tumblers.

And a knife to free the viscount.

CHAPTER ONE

Where a viscount gets into deeper trouble

A hidden nook on Cleveland Row
1817

G RIFFIN ALISTAIR BECKETT, fifth Viscount Kent, was about to do something most men wouldn't.

He was preparing to ask the infamous Black Widow for a favor.

Crouched under the awning of a haberdashery across the way from the Lyon's Den, Griff shivered inside his Weston-crafted coat. The legendary tailor would've been horrified to see the condition of his creation. Blood streaked the lapels and had soaked through the left sleeve until the original color of the wool was lost. The footpads who'd attacked him behind the Shoreditch warehouse had filched his purse and his timepiece, a Bainbridge worth a small fortune, before fleeing into the night.

He shivered, his breath a foggy mist riding the air. As Jimmie had promised, most of his business transactions were on the up and up. It was the places his partners chose to *do* business that might be the end of Griff. Thieves who'd decided to reorganize and take the legitimate route commonly ran into trouble with the ones sticking to dirty dealings. It was simple maths.

Throw a baffled viscount in the mix, and you were asking for bedlam.

The thing was, Griff had a temperature. High enough to worry him a bit. Time was possibly running out as most injuries, even superficial gashes from a blade, ended in infection. If he was set to perish at the tender age of twenty-seven, he needed assurance that certain outstanding items would be taken care of. In the past year, he'd restored the family coffers and restricted his troublesome brother's activities, check, check, check…but some issues remained unfinished.

In a last-ditch turn at redemption, he'd fashioned the brilliant idea of visiting Bessie Dove-Lyon, because he'd been unable, no matter how hard he tried, to forget about Wilhelmina Wright's bloody, blasted *cats*.

And Bessie was the only person in London he trusted.

The gaming hell's pale blue façade glimmered in the moonlit haze, the side door opening as the Lyon's Den staff finished their shifts, their footpads against damp cobbles echoing along the lane. First was the harpist, her case thumping her thigh as she disappeared into the miasma. She was followed by the dealers, Peter, Nick, Tom, and Robin, as they tumbled out in a pack, laughing and bumping shoulders. The manager, Titan, was the last to leave, checking the locks before giving Snug, the heavy standing guard for the remainder of the night, a slap on the back before ambling off.

It might be easiest to circle around to the garden entrance. Puck usually worked that door, and he and Griff had caroused once upon a time, two young bucks without a lick of sense between them. However, Snug wasn't a bad bet, and he was the *closet* bet for a viscount with blood pooling in the muck beneath his feet, his wound shallow but present, throbbing in time to his heartbeat.

Besides, Griff was family.

There might be objections, but he'd be admitted.

Heck, he'd practically lived on Cleveland Row for a couple of years after his father's passing.

Pressing his hand to his ribs, he crossed the lane in a loping sprint, grimacing with each pounding stride. *Damn,* knife wounds hurt far worse than the pistol ball he'd taken to the shoulder when he was twenty. Duels were senseless anyway, that fickle countess not worth his agony.

Snug glanced up, his stance as he shoved off the brick prepared for a fight.

"It's me, Snug," he said, his voice rumbling down the passage, "Griffin Beckett." He never used his title here. The Lyon's Den wasn't a place that respected the aristocracy.

Snug's demeanor shifted in a flash, his teeth glinting as he smiled. "You are a man among men, guv. Returning when you were the first bloke, to my knowledge, to break her contract. For a month after, we tiptoed around, bloody scared we were. Mrs. Dove-Lyon isn't a creature to dally with, even if you and the Colonel were related."

Griff nodded toward the Widow's study, thinking he'd kill for a shot of whisky right now. "Is she here?"

"You'll get me in deep, letting you in without an appointment." Snug's gaze took in his sodden sleeve, the blood coursing over his fingers. "But she'd rather you die inside than the alley. Bodies bring questions the Den doesn't need. Miss Kitty shoved a baron from an upper window last month. He bit her in a place she didn't welcome."

Griff dusted his hands together in a show of gratitude. Which cost him. Dots marred his vision, and he braced his shoulder on the brick to steady himself.

"*Hell's teeth,* guv, what have you done this time?" Snug opened a series of locks, then shoved the door open.

Griff stumbled into the vestibule, shading his eyes from the bright glow of the sconces lining the hall. "I saved my birthright through my machinations, that's what."

"Aye, no devious matchmaking for you. You might think to leave that piece out."

Griff laughed weakly and saluted his old friend, following the zesty scent of tea and citrus in a meandering path down the corridor.

The owner of the Lyon's Den didn't appear surprised when he sauntered into her study, merely dropping her quill to the escritoire, her veil fluttering with a spent breath. He took the first armchair he met and sprawled into it. A fine line of sweat was breaking out across his brow and his back. He surely looked a fright, but there was no way around it.

"Not many viscounts begin business ventures in Shoreditch," she murmured, retrieving her quill and dipping it in the inkwell at her side. "You're the most determined to escape marriage of any devil I've yet to meet. And I've met thousands. I don't take broken promises lightly, Kent."

Exhausted, Griff scrubbed his fist over his eyes, his adventure this day finally getting the best of him. "It isn't that, and you know it."

"You've always protected him."

Griff glanced to the sideboard, which seemed too long a distance to navigate. "He's my brother. What else could I do, Bessie?"

"You ruined your reputation to salvage his. He made such a mess of things I wasn't certain you could right the ship. I want you to know I didn't allow him to spend so much as a shilling after the night you dragged him away. He lost almost five thousand pounds on that gambit. However, despite my barring him here, the Lyon's Den is not the only game in Town. There are many places to bankrupt oneself."

Griff willed her to remove the veil and look him in the eye. He'd seen her once, years ago, a passing glimpse while he was roaming the halls that neither had ever mentioned. The *ton* might be startled at what they'd find beneath her cover. "My father was particularly hard on Dominic, or his abuse affected me less, take your pick. Whatever the circumstances, I'm my brother's protector. My role is firmly established, and there's no changing course."

"You're stronger," she said, tapping the quill on the desk. "The cleverest of the bunch. My favorite of my husband's cheerless family. It's why I'd hoped for more from you."

"Maybe not this time." When she raised a brow, he pressed his hand to the injury pulsing below his ribs. "I'm running a fever. The wound isn't considerable, but I don't seem to be improving. You know how infections are, speedy death and all that. Already, my mind is a bit muddled. I needed to get here before I lost reason."

"I assumed it was another silly injury from racing carriages down Bond." Mrs. Dove-Lyon swore and shoved from her chair, crossing to him. "Am I supposed to be flattered that you came to me?"

Griff tunneled his hand in his coat pocket and came out with a bloodstained list he'd hastily composed. "I trust you. There aren't many I can say that about in this town. Also, you're rumored to have medical knowledge gifted from your mother."

She ripped the crumpled sheet from his hand. "You have cheek, Griffin Alistair Beckett. True gall. After the tangle you left me with last year, that unfortunate girl and an empty chapel. If you didn't remind me so much of my Sandstrom, I would—" Releasing a tight breath, she stalked to the sconce and tilted the slip of foolscap into the light.

Griff dropped his head back, his thoughts drifting. He did *not* feel well. "I was detained the day of the wedding. Rope tying me to a chair in a rookery storeroom detained. I didn't mind marrying the chit, truth be told."

"Because she's wealthy." She sounded furious about the type of arrangement she orchestrated every day. Women with blunt and men desperately without. It was the way of their world.

"Because she's beautiful." And spirited. Intelligence shining in eyes he recalled being the color of amethyst. There'd been a palpable sweetness there, something humane and compassionate. He'd not met many kindhearted people, and he hardly knew what to make of one when he did.

He'd always yearned, a fantasy perhaps, to be connected to something or someone *good*.

The Black Widow jabbed his list at him like she held a saber. "You dragged yourself here this eve to have me tell Miss Wright you're sorry for leaving her at the altar?"

He gestured to the sheet. Dammit, that was *not* the first thing he'd written. It had to be at least the fifth. "If I pass from infection, get in touch with Dom. There are ledgers in my study, top drawer, that he'll need. Your solicitors can work with mine to steady the ship. Stay with him until he's on the right path. Which may be forever." He took a shallow breath, the skin around his wound tingling like it was on fire. "Promise me this, Bessie."

Mrs. Dove-Lyon strode to the door, rang a bell, then had a hushed conversation with a servant Griff couldn't see in the corridor. She was back in seconds, the bloodstained sheet crushed in her fist. "You think to die and let Dominic gain the title? He'll run it down within a year, into the ground. The Kents will be no more. And what about this new venture of yours, rail engines and such? Quite successful, I'm hearing. You want to abandon it when it's finally becoming lucrative?"

Griff blinked, the light in the room dimming. "Thanks, but I don't need encouragement to survive. I'd like to continue scraping along, if I can."

"For family, for my dear Colonel, I erred in judgment, and look where that got me," she whispered, her veil quivering.

"I've always believed it a hidden trait about you, a little spice you covertly add to your matchmaking. You aren't as daunting as you appear. Take my case, for instance. You thought the Wright chit suited me." He shrugged halfheartedly. "Maybe she did."

His aunt flung his list at him, and he watched it flutter to the floor. However, her touch was gentle on his brow. "You presume I'm a romantic? You must be fevered beyond comprehension. I'll help you to save my skin, Kent, to protect the Lyon's Den, as I can't have another titled cad expiring on the premises. But that's *all* it will be."

Blessedly, her heated vow was the last thing Griff heard.

HE WAS QUITE a piece to look at.

Even when he was fighting for his last breath.

"There must be another solution," Mina offered and stepped closer to the carriage, deciding it was indeed Griffin Beckett sprawled across the velvet squabs, dead to the world.

But from the steady rise and fall of his chest, not dead, *dead*.

Five minutes before, a hulking servant of the Black Widow's had knocked on her door, then directed her to the fog-laden alley behind her Limehouse terrace. A dwelling no one in London aside from her solicitors and several select clients knew existed. She didn't want to ask how Mrs. Dove-Lyon had accessed this private fragment of her life, she truly didn't.

Mina peered into the sleek black conveyance, recording the rasping breath of the man she'd planned to marry eight months prior. Muted moonlight was a splash across the long legs hanging off the seat. His face was densely stubbled, his clothing clean but clearly not his own. He didn't look anything like a viscount with one of the oldest titles in England. "Is he going to live?"

Mrs. Dove-Lyon snapped her fingers, and two strapping footmen dressed in drab clothing that wouldn't announce any connection to the Lyon's Den approached, everyone ignoring that Mina hadn't agreed to this request. "The wound wasn't ghastly, but it had become infected. My physician, the best in London, treated him and feels he'll be fine with rest. We gave him enough laudanum to keep him calm for at least a day."

Mina backed away from the carriage as they lifted him out of it. "But here? He'll recuperate *here*?"

Mrs. Dove-Lyon gave an impatient shrug. "I can't keep him at the Lyon's Den. Back to his Hanover Square manse isn't an option because I'm not sure what trouble he's gotten himself into. Until I do, it's best he remain where no one will locate him." Her veil shifted as she turned her head, looking directly at Mina. "This certifies, does it not? Who will find him in a hidden locale where you meet the thugs you work for?"

"But—"

"You owe me, Miss Wright, for the months of wasted effort I've put into obtaining a proper groom."

"They're not thugs, they're entrepreneurs." Mina followed the Black Widow and her men as they carried him gingerly through the domestic's entrance of her Georgian terrace and down the narrow corridor. "Mrs. Dove-Lyon, the man left me standing in a dusty medieval chapel with a wilted posy in my hand. Is it uncharitable to say I don't wish to associate further with him?"

"He no longer needs marriage as he's secured funds in other ways. You're safe from his attention."

"Last door on the left," Mina said, shutting the main behind them. And safe wasn't a word she'd ever use to describe Griffin Beckett. "Watch out for the rip in the runner!"

Mrs. Dove-Lyon directed them into a sitting room housing a brocade sofa Mina prayed was large enough to contain Kent's broad body. This was a modest residence, bedchamber and parlor upstairs, study and tiny kitchen on the ground floor. It hadn't been purchased for entertaining, although she quite adored it. She used it for meetings. Her neighbors would fall out of their Louis VX armchairs if her unsavory clients showed up at her family home on Regent Square.

When the motley group had the viscount settled, his head atop a pillow with a scene of Blackfriars Bridge stitched into the covering, and a threadbare blanket Mina had located partially covering him, Mrs. Dove-Lyon stepped back, assessing the scene. "This will do for now."

"May I ask why you're helping him? After what he did to both of us?"

The Black Widow's veil shook with her sigh. "I let his melancholy family life alter my judgment."

So, she cared somewhere in that leaden heart of hers.

Mina smoothed her hand down her bodice, striving to tame her racing heartbeat. Why couldn't this curiously intriguing creature who'd abandoned her at the altar be forever removed from her life? What had she done to deserve this? It seemed unfair for a woman who tried to be agreeable to her fellow human beings. "I'm supposed to have dinner with Langston on Thursday. I can't stay here for days at a time, alone with a notorious philanderer. I'm not equipped for visitors, you understand. I only have minor foodstuff and a cleaning woman who comes once a week."

"I'll have supplies sent. And someone who can serve as a chaperone. Miss Rose has decided to leave the, um, profession and is seeking other employment. This could be a trial start." The Black Widow snapped her fingers at the footman and strode into the hallway, intent on leaving Mina with *this*. "Congratulations on securing Langston, by the by. You've turned down everyone I've recommended since the debacle at the chapel and now, without assistance, landed yourself a duke. Perhaps I should ask you to work for me."

Mina raced to catch up to the trio tromping down the passageway. "I haven't landed anyone. I met him at Gunter's. I dropped my spoon, and he retrieved it for me. Then we had tea and talked all afternoon. His sister was with us, in the event you're wondering."

Mrs. Dove-Lyon halted by the door, her men having already reached the carriage. "That sounds like a horrid play on Drury. Duke

Meets Wife Over Dropped Spoon."

"There's no understanding with His Grace. Please continue sending me notes on suggested grooms. A duke isn't going to step as low as he'd have to with me."

"Hmm..." The Black Widow perched her shoulder on the door-jamb and adjusted her veil. "I don't arrange love matches, Miss Wright. You're aware of this, are you not?"

Mina recoiled, stumbling back. "I'm seeking a *business* arrangement. I've only turned down your recommendations because the men weren't the right solution to my problem." She shook her head, desperate to convey this assertion. "I don't want love."

The matchmaker laughed lightly, walking away. Over her shoulder, she murmured, "Are you sure about that?"

CHAPTER TWO

Where a viscount strives to make amends

THE SOUND OF water slapping a dock in the distance dragged Griff from sleep. He turned his head, the embroidered pillow scratching his cheek.

Where in the hell was he?

Shifting to his elbow, the tenderness in his ribs brought everything back. Being robbed in the alley behind his warehouse, then staggering to the Lyon's Den to guarantee someone had his final directives should they need them. He wasn't sure about much, but he was confident he could trust Bessie Dove-Lyon. God knows, he couldn't keep vital information with his brother, which made dying and leaving the coxcomb the title a grand fiasco.

Griff drew a breath laced with sulfur and the crisp scent of the Thames, thinking how much he loved working near the docks with his new venture. So much so he'd considered buying a residence in Shoreditch and shocking society with the decision to live amongst the rabble. The Rookery Rake Hides Out. Or, the Villainous Viscount Moves Down. The scandal rags would love it.

The woolen blanket covering him had fallen to the floor, and someone had given him tea during the night. Now cold to the touch, the cup sat on a filigree table shoved next to the sofa. He greedily drank what remained, needing about a gallon more, as his gaze shot around the room, seeking clues to ascertain his location. Shabby landscapes of coastal scenes lined the walls. A well-worn desk piled with papers and inkpots sat in a dank corner. Ledgers were scattered across the faded rug, one lying near his spent coverlet. Swinging his feet to the floor, he reached for it with a grimace.

The sheet of paper he yanked free was overflowing with calculations. Incredible sums of money totaled in neat, numerical rows, with notes in the margin in a precise, *feminine* script detailing errors in the accounting. He frowned and drew the scrap closer. The page outlined shipping expenses, and although he wasn't a smuggler, many items listed were contraband. *W.L.W. Investigations* was stamped in black across the top, an enterprise he'd never heard of.

He sensed another's presence, the scent of jasmine and ink reaching in to sting his nose. Glancing up, he found Wilhelmina Wright of the lost wedding perched in the doorway, neither in nor out. Ready to flee or toss the plate of food she held at him, he couldn't say.

"Hello, Willie," he murmured while thinking, *Ah, Bessie, bloody hell, you didn't.*

"She did." That the chit could read him so well had been a thing about her he *hadn't* liked the first time they met.

Without further comment, she stalked into the chamber, a raggedy parlor of some sort, exchanging the plate of food for the felonious sheet he held. Her gown was drab but tucked wonderfully around her reed-slim body. Enough enticement to have him sitting up straighter to get a better look.

"Eat," she ordered, then went to her haunches, gathering ledgers in her arms and out of view.

He was too hungry to argue but too curious to shut up. He gestured to the pile of criminality she was struggling to contain with his cucumber sandwich. "Is this the business Mrs. Dove-Lyon hinted at but wouldn't disclose? That you're the first female smuggler in the history of England? No wonder she felt the need to warn me." He chewed, swallowing slowly. "An outlaw viscountess, that would be novel."

Letting out a faint expletive, she hit him with a fierce look that stole his breath. *Christ*, she was stunning. Her face was near perfect, in his opinion. Delicate features with eyes so dark a violet he could almost see his frayed visage reflected there. A mulishly set mouth in startling contrast to the freshness of her beauty. Curves, but not overpowering ones, his favorite kind, flowing down to adorable, slim, *bare* feet.

She wiggled her toes at the touch of his gaze, charming him more than he'd been charmed in, well, forever. "There have been many female smugglers, pirates even, if you'd simply read a *book*, my lord."

Surprising himself, he laughed, choking on his food. Wiping his hand over his lips, he polished off another sandwich in two bites. "Where the blazes am I? On the docks, from what I can hear *and* smell."

"Limehouse Reach. Narrow Street."

He chewed, assessing the dwelling with a thoughtful eye. One of the smaller warehouses being converted to residences for the courageous few willing to acquire them. Someday, he bet this little nook would be worth a mint. "Near the Grapes, perchance?" He'd been to the famed public house on more than one occasion when the evening took him to the lower reaches. His only experience with opium, never to be repeated, had occurred there.

She clutched her illegal imports to her chest, unwilling to answer.

"Come now, Willie"—he grabbed a scone and bit into it, the sharp taste of cinnamon flowing over his tongue—"we were going to be married, sharing all this and more." The *more*, he'd been fondly looking forward to.

She shoved to her feet, the air ringing with her oath.

Griff sat back, a tad stunned, wondering how in the world he'd let this chit escape him. Beauty, brains aplenty—if the notes in the margins were hers. A woman who didn't mind the occasional swear word. A delicate flush crossed her face at the mention of intimacy, meaning she'd thought about it, too.

She was perfect.

And he'd let her slip away.

Or better to say, he'd been forcibly kept from taking her.

"I'm sorry for not showing for our wedding. I wanted, that is, I was detained." Clumsiness wasn't typically a part of his speeches to the opposite sex. He was usually smooth, mostly because he didn't care. He'd even been called glib on occasion.

Willie dumped the ledgers to the desk, her gaze when it met his, fiery hot. "You were detained until this very minute?"

Ah, she was angry. Although cross women made him cagey, he had no choice but to blunder on when the error was his. "By the time I could have made it to you, two days had passed, and I was slightly worse for wear. Bruised skin, torn clothing, foul stench. Not presentable for apologies. I sent a note to Mrs. Dove-Lyon to try and arrange a meeting, but she ignored me, which I can't blame her for, either."

"Yet you ran to her when you were in trouble last night."

"Family," he said and attacked another scone. They were damn good. "The only one in the lot I can trust."

Willie pressed her hand to her temple like she was forcing back a wave of pain.

"Aunt, by marriage. Distant but..." He shrugged, realizing this information complicated the situation. "Through the Colonel. It counts with her. And with me, I suppose, when it comes down to it."

She exhaled and propped her lovely round bum on the desk, beaten.

"She likes you," he offered because he believed this to be true.

"She would never have tossed us into her matchmaking teapot together if she didn't."

Willie placed her hand over her belly, and the gesture warmed him in a thousand ways. Vulnerability and strength were fabulously enticing traits. And that face of hers...a pure gut punch. Making him want to traverse the room and do wicked things to her, *with* her. Lay her down on the decrepit carpet and have her shout her pleasure to the gods. Slide inside her so slowly, feeling every shift and twitch of her body until they were breathless with longing. Begging for release. It had been too long since he'd lost himself in someone, forever, maybe.

His cock shifted in his trousers, in complete agreement with the fantasy.

He paused, a curious sensation sweeping him as he watched her fidget with every trinket on her colossal cherrywood desk. Had she, despite the desperate-to-find-a-husband act, *wanted* to marry him? If he'd had any clue she was warm to the idea of being his viscountess— truly not minding or even *slightly* looking forward to it—he'd have run to her straightaway once he'd gotten free of Jimmie Bean's rigging.

Because, to his mind, he seemed a poor bargain.

Willie grabbed a quill Griff reckoned she had no intention of using and twirled it in her hand. He hoped she wasn't thinking of stabbing him with it. "Why are you always embroiled in scandal? Missed weddings, which, thankfully, no one knows about. Overturned carriages, falls from terraces whilst fleeing cuckolded husbands. Being dumped in the rookery, a wound consistent with that of a blade oozing blood upon your fine clothing. Imposing on a woman you left at the altar because you can't return home due to the danger."

Griff paused mid-bite. So that's the story his aunt had cooked up to get him here. Give him a second chance with this chit, forced proximity and all. *Bravo, Bessie.* He gazed around the lackluster parlor, thinking it wasn't wholly unsuited to seduction. Still willing to toss his hat in this ring, he ticked off his motives. He was attracted. *Very*. She was willing. *Possibly.* He'd seen the spark of compassion in her eyes, no mistake, which could be a blessed thing for a scoundrel who wanted to be better than he was.

Griff frowned, his reasoning diving deeper than he'd wanted it to.

He was lonely, had always been lonely. Not a soul to call his own his entire life. He'd been years older than his siblings and shipped off to Rugby before getting to know them—and never being invited to return. He wanted a family. *There*, he'd admitted it. He wanted children and a chance to prove he could do a better job than his father had. And love. He wanted love. Or, at the very least, fondness.

Perhaps this was a way to erase those bleak memories?

What if he were allowed a real marriage, not simply a business arrangement?

Staring at Wilhelmina Wright, Griff tried to imagine such a compelling chit falling for a down-on-his-luck-but-striving-to-succeed viscount. It didn't seem possible, but she hadn't wed anyone else yet when Bessie had certainly offered alternatives to correct the mess he'd made. She likely had a list as long as her arm of suitable blokes.

Reaching up, killing him with one swift strike, his fantasy unfurled the mass of flaxen hair at her nape and shook it out with a sigh. It poured down her shoulders, *poured*, like golden cream he longed to bathe in.

"Headache," she murmured and rubbed her neck while he smoldered.

His want was fierce. An undeniable twist in his belly, the kind of emotion one couldn't ignore. Those gut inclinations that told you: this one. Pick this one. Don't think, *do*. Surprisingly, possession was there, absurdity that wrecked a man. Yet, he couldn't forget that for two weeks, between his proposal and the missed nuptials, this chit had been his.

"I can't go back. Not yet," he lied without hesitation. If nothing else, he'd have a minor respite by the docks with the most fascinating creature in England. A woman no one else had had the wits to snatch up, the fools. "The Shoreditch warehouse and my terrace in Hanover Square are being watched. Bes—um, Mrs. Dove-Lyon will alert me when I can return home. Plus"—he palmed his brow—"I'm still a tad shaky."

Working with his performance, his stomach chose that second to emit a ferocious growl. If his gaze drifted weakly to the empty plate, it couldn't be helped.

Repeating her oath, his almost-wife marched across the parlor, grabbed the dish and exited in a show of poised vexation.

This was when Griff realized Willie Wright would make the finest viscountess in the history of Kent.

HE'S A CAD, Mina fumed as Griffin Beckett flipped through her copy of *Emma*. She doubted he appreciated Austen, he seemed more a William Blake sort. Free verse and frivolity.

His sleeves were rolled to the elbow, exposing remarkably sturdy forearms, his hair a dark disorder on his head. His boots were by his side, and his feet, though covered by stockings, were long and slim. Well-shaped, like that sculpture she'd seen in the British Museum. Probably the most attractive set of feet in London, a reality sitting out there merely to spite her.

He glanced up as if he sensed her examination, his gaze shimmering, his eyes so bloody blue they made her ache. The rich, absorbing color of rogue waves ripping across the sea. Of aquamarine with bursts of sunlight shooting through their centers. Of bluebells and lapis lazuli.

Of things one knew would be dangerous—but the call to indulge was overpowering.

Flipping a page, he casually asked, "What's the L stand for?"

She let her quill droop until the ink-laden point grazed the desk. In the two hours since he'd woken, they hadn't moved from the parlor that served as her study because there was nowhere else to house the man. She had a bedchamber—*hers*—and a minuscule kitchen that couldn't even rightly be called a kitchen. While he was quickly raiding that space of its contents. Mrs. Dove-Lyon had better come through on her promise of more rations, or they'd be reduced to eating foolscap soon. "Come again, Kent?"

Amused, his lips tilted. The lopsided smile and glimmering gaze combined with that long body sprawled across her sofa presented quite the masculine portrait.

She hated that she found the viscount attractive, the craving to *touch* silent but resounding, a pulse beneath her skin and through her veins. She had a little experience in this area from her father's grooms, stolen kisses and the like, which was minor but factual. She recognized the chemical concoction weighing the air, making breathing hard.

She didn't think she mistook that he felt it, too.

Complications on all sides if she admitted to wanting him when he'd rejected her in the cruelest way possible. Only to turn around and have him perversely want her back. She scowled. *Men.*

He gestured to the stationery scattered across her desk. "L? W.L.W. Investigations."

Tell him, Mina. Tell him everything. At least this time, he didn't ask after your cats. "Laurel."

He hummed, nodded, glanced to the book. "Mine is Alastair."

Mina tapped the quill on her palm, her temper sparking. "It's quite successful."

"I'm sure it is," he murmured, failing to look up.

"I have a gift for numbers."

He lazily turned a page.

"Forensic maths, some call it. I find errors in accounts, like a detective but with calculations. The balance books are often as corrupt as the enterprise. My current project is reviewing statements for Buster McGowen. He's intent on purchasing a shipping concern from someone who is doctoring the earnings reports to increase the bids."

Griff's head snapped up, his face wiped clean of indifference. "McGowen?" The book sprawled open on his lap. "He's a gangster. A common criminal."

His incredulity made her very, very happy. "He's a businessman, like the one you're rumored to be partnering with. Jimmie Beans, isn't it? I've done several jobs for him. He's trustworthy if you can believe it. For a miscreant."

"That's different." Griff sat up quickly, then winced and grabbed his side. "A woman shouldn't engage with these sorts of characters. I'm trying to enter into only legitimate ventures myself. I merely followed an opportunity that led me to the stews. After being bound and gagged and dragged there first. Hence, the missed wedding."

Mina had heard such rubbish her entire life. Women shouldn't walk this way, talk this way, contradict men, discuss politics, wealth or social reform. No riding along Rotten Row before this hour or after that one. Rebuffed if you showed a hint of ankle or made a noise while sneezing. Forget about voicing an opinion that differed from a man's.

She was willing to marry to make things easier on herself—she understood the actual rules were never going to change—but she wasn't willing to let the rules break her. "My ventures are legitimate as well. I only point out miscalculations. It isn't my concern if the documents I review involve dubious dealings. I've found rookery types to be more respectful of my expertise than anyone in society would be."

His lips parted, and the urge to halt the flow of words with her own was overpowering. Griffin Beckett might be surprised to learn she knew how to kiss. Maybe she'd storm over there and show him.

"So, this is why you want to marry." He slumped back, cradling his ribs. "As cover for your illicit business. Or better yet, someone to manage it."

She slapped the quill to the desk, her inclination to kiss this egotistical oaf evaporating. "I don't need administration of any business but my father's. Truthfully, I have no interest in Wright's Grand Derby. I hope my husband *will*."

"But horses are amiable creatures."

Mina laughed, charmed despite herself. "So are thugs."

Griff rocked forward, ready to debate, when the knock sounded. He was up before she could reach the desk, holding his arm out and limping slightly. "I've got it. You stay put."

She started to argue—this was her house, after all—then she folded back into her chair with a sigh. She had no meetings scheduled. It was probably a runner delivering supplies, possibly the promised food.

Apparently, Viscount Kent was the protective type.

Mina sat stewing in this deduction. Mrs. Dove-Lyon had mentioned his attempts to save his family from ruin due to his brother's foolishness. It was an admirable trait, like cream for the kitten for a woman who'd never had anyone protect her. Certainly not her father. He'd not been home enough to notice a thing about her.

Griff was back in minutes, the expression on his face perplexed, his arms full of flowers.

Uh-oh. There was one domestic, a footman of long-standing in her family who knew about the Limehouse dwelling. He delivered mail and any items Mina might need immediately with her investigations. Why a bouquet had made the list of must-haves, she couldn't say.

She scrambled to reach the viscount before he read the card, but he was faster, holding it above her head. He shoved the tulip-laden arrangement at her, a floral wall between them.

"Until Thursday," he read, his dark brow winging high. "Langston." His lips rolled down as he repeated the name. When it met hers, his gaze was as frosty as a windowpane in February. His eyes were indeed the bluest blue she'd ever seen. "As in, Duke of?"

Clutching the bouquet, Mina ripped the card from his grasp. "As if it's any of your affair."

"It was nearly my lifelong affair."

Skirting him, she entered the hallway, heading for her petite kitchenette. There was a cracked vase in the cupboard if she remembered correctly. "I'm not discussing this with a man who failed to show up for our wedding. Once you're no longer shaky and your residences not being watched, you're free to leave."

"I told you, I was detained. Rope-tied-to-chair detained. I apologized sincerely."

She felt him behind her, his body heat an imposition she longed to sink into.

"Langston," he murmured as if he couldn't believe it. "Blimey, Bessie went for the highest reaches in her next attempt. I feel slighted."

Mina dumped the bouquet on the scuffed timber counter and shot Griffin Beckett a sly side glance from beneath her lashes. "I caught this one on my own. Innocently, over tea at Gunter's." Laughing, she bounced on her toes, reaching for the vase. "I dropped my spoon."

"Is that the way to locate a wife in Town these days? By recovering lost utensils in tea shops?"

"Gentlemen retrieve spoons and show up for weddings."

When she turned, having crammed the flowers in a container that didn't match their beauty, he was there, caging her between his broad body and the counter. A jolt of yearning swam through her, so rare a sensation it frightened her. She appreciated the male form and wasn't above subtly studying a man she found attractive. But she'd rarely, *rarely*, had the thrill turn her knees to jelly, snatch her breath and twist it in her lungs.

Or make her visualize what came after kisses. Matters unfamiliar but unexpectedly desired.

"You had your chance, Kent."

Catching her jaw, he tilted her head until their gazes clashed. "Marry him then. You'll make a fine duchess. Reach for the stars, I respect the decision." Leaning, his lips grazed hers, a feather-light caress that did all kinds of wonderful things to her. "But for now, in a clandestine nook by the docks, kiss the lowly viscount who wants you like he's never wanted anyone in his life."

It was a request Mina hadn't the power to refuse.

He swept her away with elegance, not authority. Stepping in with a move so gentle, she yearned for a rougher charge. Lacking room to negotiate, they were obliged to seek steadiness in each other. Her hands glided over his shoulders, fingers sinking into the silky strands at his nape. His hands caught her hips and pulled her into him.

Lips parting, tongues caressing before diving into a frantic dance.

What started tenderly, quickly spun away from them, the attraction bouncing like a ball about the parlor earlier, roaring to life. The air thickened, charged with passion, heating until it sizzled like before a storm.

Or perhaps that was merely her body going up in flames.

The kiss was unlike any she'd experienced. The incidents with her father's grooms—two, in fact—behind Wright's main stable were laughable in comparison. Heart-pounding, skin-flushing awareness rolled through her, the rush coming out in a tattered sound that did something desperate to the man holding her. His mouth forcefully seized hers, any hint of civility exhausted, his hand moving up to cup her breast, his thumb seeking her achingly hard nipple through layers she wanted removed immediately.

Groaning, Griff took her to another place, a deep, dark, decadent place.

Now. *This*. Here.

They bumped bodies, grasping, fingers tangling in clothing and hair. His staggered breaths struck her cheek, her teeth nipped his jaw.

She followed, each fragment of his pleasure hers to match. It was a glorious time to find she was a competitive soul, unwilling to let her "lowly" viscount win this battle. She tried to tell him, harsh whispers against his lips, but he pulled her words into his throat, kissing her until her vision dimmed.

The most mysterious, wondrous element was the rigid shaft pressed against her belly. The contact with her father's grooms had not included this.

Dear heaven, she wanted to look, touch, break him with her passionate fury.

Tracking the urge, Mina was reaching for his cock when he caught her wrist, his exhalation coming out in a feral burst against her neck. "Stop it, Wilhelmina Laurel Wright. Or I'm going to forget myself, lift you to a counter that doesn't look strong enough to hold us and tup the breath from you while I balance you atop it. They'll hear our shouts at the docks, I swear to you, they will. I won't let up for *one* second until your cries of ecstasy reach the clouds."

She panted and gave him a shove that, in his dazed state, sent him skipping back. "Why do you sound angry"—her hand shot out, gesturing between them—"after this?"

He glanced away, disconcerted. Yanked his hand through his hair and muttered a string of nonsensical words before his gaze fired back to her. "Because…I know…that is, you've done this before."

Her laughter came out in a choking gasp. *Oh*, he must be joking. "So have you! A thousand times, according to reports."

His chest rose and fell, his jaw flexing. He shoved his hands in his trouser pockets—to keep them off her, she suspected. "How many?"

She released a breath that shot through her teeth. "How many for you?"

"It's different for me, Willie." And, of course, he had no idea.

"You're troubled because I have scant experience, but some experience, when you have leagues. To vex you further, I'll let you wonder how much I have and with whom. A bit hypocritical, Kent, when you're going to have to start roaming remote villages because you've tupped everyone in London." She chewed on her lip, pleased to her bones when his mouth tensed as he stared, his aggrieved sigh streaking past her. "Though jealousy becomes you."

He took a step back. "I'm *not* jealous."

She turned to the flowers and began hastily arranging them to avoid launching herself into his arms or bashing him over the head with her cracked vase. If she had to lean into the counter because her knees shook, she could easily hide this fact. "Fine, then. Since you have no objection, Thursday with Langston stands."

"I already told you to marry the man. Not often a chit gets a duke on the hook. The craftiest matchmaker in England could only secure you a measly viscount."

"Since you're up to this bit, you're capable of recovering without supervision," she said, stung, shoving her hurt deep. *What had she expected?* "You can stay here until it's safe, but I'm going home. I'll ensure supplies are delivered, but that's the last I'm willing to do for you."

This said, Mina walked away, not about to tell him that his kiss had been one from her dreams.

CHAPTER THREE

Where a viscount makes sense of a confounding situation

H E WASN'T JEALOUS.

Viscounts who'd made a run through the chits in London in the manner he had didn't get jealous. They got smarter. They learned their lessons. They protected their hearts. They controlled the affair.

They decided the when, the where, *and* the why.

Jealousy was for green lads and broken blokes. Jealousy was for men who ended up walking the love plank. Griff wasn't walking that plank, ever. Not after watching what so-called affection had done to his parents. A fond union he'd agree to. He believed it would make life more amicable—happy wife, happy life and all that.

Blind devotion? He dusted his hands on his trousers. No, thank you.

Griff circled the parlor—his prison because he'd lied to Willie about being in danger—trying to outline a plan for success.

Only he wasn't sure what he wanted to win.

The girl or the argument?

Should he never speak to her again? Or lock her in his bedchamber and pleasure her until she couldn't voice so much as one complaint?

The last option seemed promising but perilous. He liked her a bit *too* much to depend solely on amorous relations. The fond sensation circling his chest was new—and unwelcome.

Feelings could, he acknowledged, be deadly.

Cursing beneath his breath, he halted before one of the horrid paintings lining the walls. A pastoral scene created by a genuinely ungifted artist. If he stuck it in the grimy alley behind the building, how long would it take for it to walk away? Maybe never. That might be a fun game he could play to burn time until the chit he feared he was infatuated with chose to check on him. Because she was planning to check on him, wasn't she?

He'd already stroked himself to completion. Twice, while thinking of that kiss and what he'd longed to do after it. Willie Wright had a surprisingly shapely body hidden beneath those ugly gowns. In a short span of time, he'd created some vivid pictures in his mind of his almost-wife sprawled across silk sheets. Riding him in his carriage. Against the wall in the stables. Atop a bench in the conservatory at the Hertfordshire estate he'd always wanted to have a go at.

Ah, the many places one could tup when one found the right person.

Griff frowned. Right was the wrong word, although he couldn't come up with something better.

It'd been two days since she stormed from her secreted flat on the docks. Two long, irrefutably lonely days.

When Griff could have returned home himself. His wound was healing, still painful, but the puckered skin around the gash was a paler shade of crimson. Luckily, he'd found a lad on the street willing to make a shilling, and his work had been delivered to him. Waiting for her to come back seemed silly, but he guessed that was what he was doing. He didn't want her to know he'd lied in addition to missing their nuptials.

Good to her word, she'd had foodstuff and newspapers delivered, a book even. William Blake, whom he quite liked. But not a peep else. Not a glimpse of those glorious violet eyes. A hint of that sly, kind smile. A moment of wicked wit shared.

While the kiss circled his mind, roaming like a ravenous tigress, sinking its teeth in.

A kiss from his dreams. He'd never experienced the like, wrapped up in a woman in *seconds*. Lost to this world. A goner.

Body reacting to the lewd visions filling his head, Griff straightened the painting with an irritated flick. He could marry her. Ask her straightaway, with a ring and everything. He had a stunning piece stashed in his top desk drawer, a sapphire with this purplish tint he'd picked out after meeting her. It wasn't as gorgeous as her eyes, but it was close. In fact, it had been in his waistcoat pocket the day of his kidnapping.

He'd show up to the ceremony this time, no worries on her part.

Yet, due to his new enterprise and the funds flowing in, he didn't need a fat dowry, not desperately. Besides, the woman in question had secured a duke.

A bloody *duke*.

Griff stalked to the desk, slumping into her chair. The air smelled faintly of female, a teasing, enticing scent. Not too heavy or too light, but simply perfect. He drew a sheet close, studying her script, the calculations littering the page. She had lovely handwriting, bold and unflinching, like the woman. Her intelligence evident in the computations.

Sighing, Griff tossed the paper to the desk. Fucking Langston. The man held a billiard stick like a babe. He couldn't play a hand of Piquet without showing the entire value of his cards on his stupid face. Griff would love to tell her he'd once been tossed from his mount during a polo match at Cambridge. That he'd almost been sent down for an incident with a mathematics professor's wife, Griff would keep to himself.

Although everyone at university knew about it.

Griff gave her quill a spin. Better, perhaps, to not share stories when your opponent had more goods on you than you had on them.

However, Langston wasn't his opponent. Griff wasn't fighting for anyone but his family. And his bloody title. And the properties, tenants, and staff dependent on him. The village roads in need of repair, the church's faulty roof. If Willie Wright wanted a duke, let her have a duke. Even if he couldn't play polo worth a shite and held a cue like an infant.

The knock was energetic enough to have Griff shoving from the chair. On the way to the front entrance, he grabbed a parasol tucked in the corner. It had a pointed metal tip that could inflict damage if one applied enough force. Thugs apparently visited this residence on the regular, and Griff's pistol was in the top drawer of his desk alongside Willie's ring.

When he opened the door, there wasn't a criminal of any sort on the step. Merely a delivery boy he'd seen around the Lyon's Den who was stomping mud from his boots and flicking hair that was much too long from his eyes.

"Lord Kent?" the lad asked, daring as you please, presenting a large parcel as if it were a royal order. He eyed the parasol with disdain. Griff grunted and took the package, then dug in his trouser pocket, thankfully finding three pence.

Tossing his weapon aside, he waited until he reached the desk before opening the box, a bit uneasy about who might know where he was. He didn't think the footpads who'd jumped him in the alley days ago had been lying in wait, but he couldn't be positively sure. He didn't want to bring trouble to Willie's door, more than she was bringing herself by collaborating with ruffians.

However, the parcel wasn't anything but another considerable shove in her direction.

A half mask and cloak were inside, a folded vellum sheet bearing the Lyon's Den stamp on top. *Miss Wright will be at this address tonight, taking her business into areas it shouldn't go. She's decided to expand her investigations beyond the purview of her accounts. Look for a pearl domino and blue satin. 10 Bow Street, St. Giles.*

"Bloody hell," Griff growled and tossed the summons to the desk. *St. Giles.*

He trailed his finger down the gold cord binding the cloak's hem. The garment was extravagant and not his style, and the mask was made of leather and certain to be uncomfortable.

The bothersome chit wasn't his problem.

Let the Duke of Langston rescue her from her blasted ambitions.

OUT OF ALL the events he'd been forced to attend, Griff hated masquerade balls most of all. He didn't like roleplaying in bed or in life. The mask indeed chafed and the voluminous cape hit him at the ankle, a monstrous piece of ridiculousness swirling like mist behind his every step.

He didn't look himself, which was the bloody point, wasn't it?

Music from a quartet flowed past as he waded through the suspiciously dressed crowd, grasping hands and leering smiles an expected part of the scenario. A pinkish sunset glow, rare to London, spilled a rosy twilight hue across the ballroom's marble floor.

Had Willie any idea what she was getting into when she'd agreed to attend? This was demimonde at its finest. He recognized a Drury actress he'd had a minor association with two years ago across the gallery. The mistress of a prince in one corner, the wealthiest courtesan in England in another. Not the kind of fete his almost-wife was typically invited to if she was invited to any. Her father's success hadn't endeared her to the *ton*, that was certain. Money spoke volumes but rarely made it to the upper reaches.

Griff began to get anxious, afraid he'd missed her when she stepped into view from the veranda's French doors.

It was awful what he experienced upon seeing her. Dreadful.

He halted in place, his cape settling around him with a beaten sigh.

Her gown was a benediction, a lustful creation that urged his cock into a painful press against his trouser buttons. An ice blue satin promise molded to her form, the daring neckline drawing every ravenous gaze in the place. She had a magnificent body, he realized sullenly. What chit with such a gifted mind needed breasts like those? The urge to toss his ridiculous cloak over her and drag her away was blinding. When she wasn't his to protect. He'd ruined that chance by deserting her in a remote chapel in the woods.

She didn't appear to notice him, and with his senseless costume in place, he wouldn't expect her to. So, he trailed her much as he had other women in other ballrooms, getting close but not too, the scent of sameness merging memories of prior conquests into one fat lump in his mind. It wasn't the ideal time to realize he was exhausted, to his bones, with those endeavors. The false compliments, the whispered suggestions, the *games*.

By God, he was getting himself on track with this business venture, lifting the Kent title from the ashes through hard work and diligence. Restoring the Beckett name. With a few minor, nearly legal cut corners, which was his way. You couldn't completely remove a man from his innate personality. He was creating something durable for the future. Mending fences with his family when they'd helped destroy them right along with him. As the eldest, responsibility for the entire jumble was riding on his shoulders.

Griff was, if nothing else, aware of his obligations.

Along that vein, he observed his almost-wife as she circled the space, dodging some appeals, halting to entertain others. Her smile was fixed and false, her gaze seeking information, not entertainment.

She had a plan, and getting tupped in the deserted parlor of a newly-minted baron's manse in St. Giles wasn't on the list. He was thankful, but every time a man touched her with so much as a gloved pinkie, his hands curled into fists at his side. She'd had two glasses of champagne at his count, certainly one more than necessary. A third she'd adeptly poured in a palm as she passed it.

The youngest son of the Earl of Dodson stopped her as she passed, his gaze dropping promptly to her bosom. He had a reputation that made Griff's look positively angelic.

Griff grabbed a flute off a passing footman's tray and tossed back the contents. This watching business wasn't going to work for much longer if Willie didn't start keeping her stunning smiles to herself.

Possession wasn't a sensation he'd embraced with any familiarity before. It chafed as badly as his mask.

At least he wasn't brainless enough to think he could control her.

But defend? Griff recalled the blade tucked at the ready in his boot. Maybe.

CHAPTER FOUR

Where a fearless woman experiences fearful feelings

D ID HE THINK she didn't know he was there?

Griffin Beckett *wasn't* an able detective, she decided as she crept down the corridor in search of a painting. Light from the oil sconces drifted over the Aubusson runner at her feet, the excess illumination witness to the homeowner's wealth. Mina would never hire a viscount should her business expand into investigations outside accounts containing erroneous calculations. The moment he entered the ballroom, the hair on the back of her neck had risen, her skin prickling unnervingly.

She didn't appreciate what her body was trying to tell her.

Anyway, it was futile for him to try to hide. One, he was practically the tallest man in the room. Two, masks didn't conceal eyes the color of vast oceans and sunny skies. Three, *oh*...she groaned and halted before the door the footman she'd bribed had told her was the baron's study.

Three was all about *him*.

Viscount Kent had that intangible talent, the rare few were gifted at birth. Magnetism that went above and beyond. Women were drawn to it, men envious but admiring. Where some held it high, like a carrot out of reach, Griff shared his charm with his lazy smiles and occasional winks. *Winks.* Mina growled and gave the study's beveled glass doorknob a hard twist. He'd winked at the woman, an actress if Mina wasn't mistaken, who'd blocked him at the edge of the ballroom floor, the silk chiffon barely covering her bosom, a blatant invitation.

Mina had decided then and there that now was the time to begin W.L.W Investigation's first non-mathematical quest. Happily, she'd inched from the ballroom before her erstwhile protector could wreak more havoc on London's female delegation. She'd been asked by a former client of absurd influence to look into a piece of art that may or may not be hanging in a certain baron's study. Either her former client wanted to steal it—or steal it *back.*

She'd not asked and did not want to know.

A modest undertaking for which she was being handsomely compensated. Uncomplicated. Safe. Mostly.

More importantly, she would then be owed a favor. Her grand plan was to have every gent of influence indebted to her. Her father's advice—hit them where it hurts—sticking. At least he'd given her something, her papa.

Thankfully, the room was unlocked. In preparation, she'd researched how to pick locks—and had practiced on her own—but hadn't any guarantee it was a skill she'd mastered. Shutting the door, she closed her eyes and leaned against it in relief. Shoving her mask atop her head, she let the chilled air strike her cheeks for the first time in hours.

Step one complete.

The sound of flint striking a tinderbox had her straightening in alarm.

"I was wondering when you'd make it, Willie. A long hallway, true, but not that long."

Mina shook her head. *No,* he couldn't possibly… How had he…

What was...

The decision was made. She was going to kill him.

With an amused grin, his ridiculous mask still in place, he shrugged and lit the lamp's wick, repositioning it on the desk with a flourish. "The footman was willing to tell me everything, although I had to pay him double what you'd given. The lad's made excellent wages tonight. In the future, my advice, increase your bribes. And put your mask back on in case someone stumbles in here and finds us, will you."

"I don't need saving," she whispered and crossed to him in a fury. The ripple of happiness was an emotion she simply *had* to conquer. "Nobody knows who I am. You're the infamous one. Save your rescuing for a girl who needs it."

He glanced around the space, then back at her, his gaze slightly, finally, touched with irritation. "I'd hardly call this a rescue. More an intervention."

She braced her hands on the desk and leaned until she could see the gold flecks swimming in sapphire. That little fact of his visage had not been her imagination. "Why are you here, Kent?"

He mirrored her pose, close enough to touch. The teasing scent of leather and a spicy fragrance all his own drifted to her. She took it in hungrily, the moment spinning out as they stared, lost. The air lit like the lamp's wick, going buttery hot. The kiss they'd shared roared through her mind, her body.

My, she thought in wonder, *he looks like he belongs in this scene of treachery and deception. And I want to belong. To someone.*

"It's not the blunt, is it?" he whispered, his voice achingly soft. His jaw flexed, his exasperated sigh splitting the air. The mask came off in a flash and was crushed in his fist. "You don't need the money, not one penny. It's the excitement. Which makes it a hundred times worse. A bored heiress with a one-in-a-million intellect. That's a combustible combination." With an oath, he yanked his cape free and let it drift to the floor. "I'm frightened of that combination."

"You hypocrite." She shoved off the escritoire, breaking his hold. "When boredom drives every decision you make." She tapped her chest, wishing she hadn't when his eyes flared. Her gown had the lowest neckline of any she'd ever owned. "Because I'm a woman, I don't get wearied? I don't want *more*? You have no idea what it's like being held back."

He rose to his full height, towering over her, the desk between them, thank heaven. He had the longest, lean-but-muscular body of any man she'd ever met. Exquisiteness that made her mouth water. Her yearning posed an argument: *see what he looks like underneath his fine clothing.*

"Your duke isn't going to give you more, Willie. Not this kind of more, if that's what you've found you require for true contentment." Shaking himself free of her hold this time, he circled the study, halting before a small painting. *The* painting, if she wasn't mistaken. Trailing his hand along the scrolled frame, he added, "Matters like this, demimonde balls and hidden rookery flats, sneaking into private domains and bribing servants about stolen artwork, require collaborators with blades in their boots. Men willing to roll the dice. Not every bloke can match you in this, I'll bet my life on it at the Lyon's Den."

"Do you have a blade in your boot, Griffin Beckett?"

He glanced over his shoulder, his smile meant to destroy her if she let it. "As a matter of fact, I do."

Raised voices in the hallway pierced the air, getting louder as the boisterous group closed in. A scuffle in the making. Mina had heard enough at Wright's to know what impending brawls sounded like.

Going on feral instinct, Griffin ripped the painting off the wall, clasped her upper arm as he strode past, yanking her through a side door and into the next chamber before she could take a breath.

"Griff," she whispered, but he immediately shushed her. "What are you—"

"Shh." Glancing about, he halted for a split-second, then was on the move again. As if he'd done this before. Nothing to figuring out how to flee with pilfered artwork jammed under your armpit.

She supposed this was his version of "rolling the dice."

The storage closet he shoved her into was microscopic and without a hint of freshness contained within. The stink of mothballs and dust permeated the space, making her gasp as he roughly backed her into the paneled wall and closed the door.

"I don't like tight confines," she whispered into the warm nook above the buttoned vee of his waistcoat. Point of fact, small spaces made her panicky and had since she was a child.

Shouts in the study, cries that unfortunately included the word *painting,* made their way to her.

Griff swore and lowered the canvas to the floor, bumping her on the way down because there was no way around it. "I'm here, Willie. Stay calm." When he straightened, her dread soared for different reasons. They were pressed like petals in a book. She had nothing to do but cling to him, one hand curled around his lean hip, the other twisted in his shirt. His heartbeat skipped beneath her wrist in a mad rhythm, daring them both.

He tilted her chin up, and in the shadows, she noted a blazing indigo glow in his eyes. Light wasn't needed to detect his arousal wedged against her. Her longing wasn't as obvious, but it was there. In the fevered breaths sliding between the layered folds of his cravat, working their way to his skin. She didn't wish to suffer alone.

"We're confused by the near miss at the chapel," he finally said, offering a weak explanation. "A connection when there isn't really a connection. Bessie's talk of marriage and forevers, even when she scarcely believes in them herself, is enough to confound anyone. Leaving me muddled, furious that you're taking such chances when they're your chances to take. Then you show up in a gown like this, one created to make men mad."

"I'm not yours," she whispered when the statement felt like a lie.

His lips found the crown of her head, her brow, her cheek. Her skin erupted, heat swimming through her at the caress. "You're not mine."

Of course, the kiss was inevitable.

A boundless fall, a devouring conquest. A show of skill, proficiency, and growing expertise.

Cupping her jaw, he directed her where he needed her to be to begin the most profound sensual invasion of her life. Her lips parted without hesitation, allowing all he sought. The glossy thickness of his hair grazed her palm as she slanted his head, taking what she wanted, too. Searching, chasing, leading. Fingertips digging into flesh, skin moist from the effort, pulses thumping. They switched roles and dominance so quickly that it made her breath cease.

Bodies finding the connection he'd spoken of, one without words.

His yearning lit a flame she didn't desire to extinguish. He was generous, giving, and at the same time, greedy. Emotions she channeled and released back to him.

The fond affection of the last encounter faded from memory as the savage strength of this one took over. Growling gently, he moved her against the wall, lifting her to her tiptoes, positioning his cock where she most wanted it, a preview of what he'd do after he climbed atop her. They explored as much as they could with layers of cloth between them. A grind, a buff, his length long and hard, almost as if he was polishing her in places, *ah*, that needed care. His lips matched the tempo until it sparked a sizzling blaze between her thighs. When his hand arrived to cup her breast, knead lightly but with intent, she curved into the possession.

The quiver swirled, feet to belly, making her break the kiss, her mouth against his neck, tormented sighs released against his flushed skin. She knew what was close to happening. She'd done it to herself in her bedchamber. Lately, while thinking of *him*.

"Don't you dare stop," she ordered into his cravat's silken creases, bowing her head and concentrating on pleasure. "Not when you've come this far, brought me here."

"Come, then." His voice was broken, the words ragged. "I've got it."

The clamor in the baron's study hadn't abated, drunken shouts and general chaos sliding under the closed door. Sounds of furniture being overturned. Someone singing a vulgar song at a high pitch. Laughter, bawdy merriment. The thump of a bottle hitting the wall.

Griff seemed to ignore it, as she was trying to. Because they couldn't leave. Furthermore, she wanted what he was offering. Above her safety. Above her reputation, which wasn't outstanding to begin with.

She finally understood the lengths people would go to for *this*.

She spread her legs when he reached, fistfuls of satin drawn to her waist, crushed in his fist. He whispered in her ear, letting her know what he was doing. Each word bringing her closer. *I'm touching here, stroking this spot. Lean into me. Close your eyes. Let go.*

She wasn't naked. A layer of silk and one of cotton separated his hands from her swollen sex, but he knew how to work around it. She wondered if he even considered it a challenge. Possibly. The glint in his eyes before her head fell back in delight was that of a man wrestling a tiger.

The bliss when it hit her was astonishing, unlike any she'd managed on her own. A fire flood of sensation cascaded down her spine, turning her body to molten bone and sinew. Her breasts ached, her core pulsed, her body seeking more but willing to accept this.

The world receded until there was nothing but Griffin Beckett's touch and her fascination.

"I want your hands on me," he growled before kissing her, capturing her low moan and pressing her back, back into the wall. His own groan traveled down her throat as he trembled.

Had he...?

She tried to catch his gaze, marveling, unsure. *Had he?*
The scent of smoke and hoarse bellows ended her questioning.
And her adventure.

CHAPTER FIVE

Where a viscount is embarrassed and enchanted

GRIFF PACED THE width of the ramshackle Limehouse parlor they'd returned to. Fled to. Having a residence no one knew about was beneficial for debacles such as these.

He sipped straight from a bottle, bypassing the tumbler he'd been given, hoping the whisky would help clear his mind—and soon. It had been ages since he'd crawled out a window, and certainly never, that he recalled, with flames leaping at his back and a pilfered canvas jammed under his arm. The woman he'd humiliated himself with, a puddle of satisfied delight at his side.

Someone to worry mightily over.

When he rarely had anyone to think of but himself.

Knocking the bottle against his teeth, he glanced at the painting perched on Willie's settee, a portrait of an old woman reading a book that he found too woeful to crave. Who needed their artwork to tell them how sad it all was? If he could afford a Rembrandt, which he couldn't. And he hated to tell the dazzling woman with her head in her hands and a glass of whisky by her side—proof of his devotion drifting lazily from her skin—that they'd filched a damned masterpiece.

"My task was not to steal it," she repeated for at least the twentieth time. Streaks of ash covered her cheeks, creating absurdly charming hollows. She looked an adorable fright. "I was simply to ensure it was *there*. Record the location and review the signature. Now we have to bloody return it. When the baron's house might not be standing after the lamp you lit got pitched to the floor in the chaos. The study is destroyed, to be sure."

"In that case, maybe it's good we filched it."

She grunted, disgusted with the situation.

"*I'll* return it," Griff ground out in a tone he hoped conveyed his inflexibility. His almost-wife wasn't returning to St. Giles, not for one second. Was it his fault those drunken fools had nearly burned down the manse? Maybe he'd ask Bessie to assist him since she'd gotten him in this tangle in a roundabout way.

She had all kinds working at the Lyon's Den. Someone to return a pinched artifact? Not a problem. Someone to separate him from a troublesome heiress, however...

He feared he didn't want to escape the clutches of Wilhelmina Laurel Wright. Instead, he wanted to be in *deeper*.

Glancing up, he felt the shift, as reliable as a church's bell tolling in his belly. A quake in the region of his heart that he'd fight to the death to deny. Thankfully, she'd removed that hazard of a gown and was now back in one of her dour specialties that adequately covered her generous breasts.

Still, the needy pulse was there beneath his skin. Lying in wait to slay him.

They'd gone to three, maybe four, on a scale of ten in that closet. As intimate a first take as any he'd encountered. He wanted the remaining six counts with Willie more than his next breath.

Although it was reckless, what they'd done. A danger to both of them.

Falling for the alluring woman he'd left at the altar wasn't happening.

"Today's Thursday," he reminded her, taking note of the crimson splashes the bountiful sunrise was lobbing across an Axminster carpet that should have been thrown in the rubbish heap years ago. He sniffed, longing for the modern bathing facilities at his townhouse. His clothing reeked of smoke, his hair standing on end from the rain they'd encountered on the way here.

"I know what day it is," she murmured against the rim of her glass.

"Your appointment is this evening." Although the thought of Langston's baby-soft hands on her made him want to put his fist through her parlor's cracked plaster. Nevertheless, solid advice was solid advice. Taking a chance on a duke was the brilliant choice. If Griff was acting the friend, and only the friend, he had to be honest.

Her gaze was scorching, a violet assault. "You mean Langston is safer because he doesn't burn down houses or steal paintings? Or leave fiancées standing in dank chapels with a sad twist of freesia in their hands." She sipped, her expression impassive, her flaxen hair a gorgeous tumble flowing over her shoulders. She had to be the most fascinating woman in England, she simply *had* to be. "I bet he doesn't carry a blade in his boot, either."

She didn't mention how Griff had touched her in the confines of that splendid little closet. How the air had lit like magnesium around them.

Therefore, he felt he must.

"I can't help it any more than you can, this thing between us." With the bottle, he gestured to her, to him, then back again. "If it makes you feel better, the situation has traveled beyond my considerable control."

"Did you have a similar reaction to that tart at the masquerade ball?"

Griff halted, bracing his hip on the sofa's cherrywood lip, facing her but far enough away that he couldn't touch. "The actress?" Unable to recall the tart's name, he laughed, realizing seconds later that this was the wrong response. His almost-wife wasn't pleased. "She means nothing to me, sweet. A chit I can barely recall when"—he lifted his hand to his nose and inhaled Willie's glorious scent in—"you're implanted in my very *being*. The smell of you on my skin, your moans sliding into my ears, your body quivering around mine. My dreams have been filled with lewd visions since the moment we met. It was the only reason I was relieved when those delinquents tied me to a chair and kept me from you because I feared the hold you had over me."

Her lips parted as she turned his admission over in her mind. Always a tough customer, she drew the moment out until it was painful.

Why had he gone and called her *sweet*? He was losing his mind.

Griff tapped the bottle against his knee. "Like you do, I want the rest. Every moaning, grasping moment with a desperation that makes me furious and frightened in turn. Like I said in the closet, I want your hands all over me. Your lips, your *teeth*, especially that front one with the little crook. How's that for honesty? But that doesn't mean I'm going to take it...or that you should give it. My being prevented from attending our nuptials was celestial intervention. We're finding our own way without it being forced upon us at the smoking end of Bessie Dove-Lyon's pistol."

Willie's gaze narrowed, and he experienced a jolt of fear at what she was about to say. "You quivered." When he didn't respond, she made a vague gesture to her lower body that had the power to send him tumbling over the edge. "When we...in the...you reacted, as I did."

The gulp of whisky burned a broad path to his gut. *Well, hell.* "That isn't typical much past boyhood. Hasn't happened to me since I was fifteen or so. My apologies." He propped the bottle on his thigh, desire flaring anew when she followed the move, her gaze lingering near his crotch. "I'm not proud of it, no man would be, but I'm not going to lie, either. I was undone."

What he *wasn't* going to admit was that he'd never been as involved in a mere kiss, so much so that he lost himself and released in his trousers. His cravat hadn't even been undone, for pity's sake. But he'd been helpless. His almost-wife had been sighing out these tiny mews against his neck, her core hot as a hearth even with a set of frilly drawers separating them. He'd never forget how her lids had drifted low, her head falling back as she came.

His weakness was wretched and, in some horridly menacing way, beautiful.

To yearn with such urgency hadn't been a part of his prior escapades. He'd been unprepared for the strength of his need.

Unfortunately, he'd provided his intrepid investigator with a riddle. "So, you have trouble controlling yourself with me but no issue controlling yourself with tarts?"

Considering, Griff hummed an off-key tune, wondering how she could look so lovely covered in soot, her hair a tragedy, her gown this side of repellent. "Likewise, as you have no issue controlling yourself with dukes. Been jammed in any closets with Langston lately?"

A minuscule pleat inserted itself between her eyebrows. The urge to cross to her and kiss it away was palpable. "You're not really in danger, are you? Mrs. Dove-Lyon made that up to keep you here. A second chance at matchmaking. This has all been a hoax, a ruse to pass the time."

He stared through the bottle, her visage golden and hazy, recognizing with a heavy heart that their time together was ending. "Not any more danger than usual."

She glanced at the painting, her chest falling with a spent breath. "Then you can leave now so we're not seen together. Before day breaks."

"Because you need to prepare for an evening with a duke who doesn't lie, steal paintings, romance tarts, miss weddings, or keep blades in his boot."

"So, it appears," she whispered.

CHAPTER SIX

Where a woman contemplates indelicate topics

I WANT YOUR *hands on me.*

Mina stared at the King's Theatre stage, wondering when those words would leave her. *I want every moaning, gasping moment.* Mozart's *The Magic Flute* flowed over her, while it was Griffin Beckett's voice she heard in her mind.

I was undone.

It had been two weeks since he'd walked out her rookery door without a passing glance. Of course, she'd given him no option to stay. Not after he'd lied. Forced proximity was only helpful if it was actually forced. True to his threat, he'd returned the painting to the underworld titan who'd hired her, fabricating a story about Mina snatching the piece off the wall when the fire started, its recovery due entirely to her quick thinking.

In the end, she'd been paid even more handsomely for her trouble while left wondering if she'd stolen a priceless canvas from its rightful owner.

The note she'd received from Lord Kent was concise, telling her what she needed to know and nothing more. *Funds for the completed task are included. Burn this missive upon reading.* If she'd been unable to dispose of a wrinkled page bearing his looping script, his charming signature—*Sincerely, G.A.B.*—this was a weakness she could easily hide beneath the blotter on her desk.

There'd been no mention of breathtaking kisses or two evenings spent in companionable conversation in a Limehouse flat. Shared histories and a glimpse into the world another inhabited. For all that she was surrounded by people in London, Mina didn't know any of them well. And no one knew her. She'd been a lonely child and was approaching being a lonely old woman.

Unless she took the duke up on his offer.

Because an offer was coming. She recognized the signs even if she wasn't experienced with such things. A chaperoned dinner at his home, two strolls in Hyde Park, also escorted, and a horrid musicale at the Earl of Williams-Firth's Mayfair terrace. And tonight, the opera. For a man who'd not made a move to kiss her, Langston had made quite the public show of courting her. It was puzzling. She was the daughter of a racetrack owner, a woman far beneath him in status.

Yet, she still needed a husband. The painting debacle had proven that she required support and some level of protection, even if she'd like to believe she didn't. Therefore, her say-yes-to-the-duke list now stood at a solid six.

Glancing at Langston from the corner of her eye, she ticked off the points on her fingers.

He was jovial.

Handsome, if a woman didn't mind being slightly taller.

Uncomplicated in the best of ways, his life wholly handled by his sister, his wife set to take over the role when she married in two months.

He had an agreeable family, deceased parents he'd loved and no baggage dragging along behind him to muck things up. (Amazingly, he didn't loathe any of his four siblings.)

He'd retained his inheritance and didn't require her money.

Mina frowned and pulled at the crooked seam of her glove. What was the last one again? Had she already mentioned his pleasant nature?

The ripple of chatter had her glancing around the theatre. There was movement directly across from the duke's box. A woman in a garish crimson gown and—

Mina sat up with an audible breath she wished she could retract.

The *cad*. The crooked, dirty bounder.

Viscount Kent made no effort to conceal his arrival—or the scandal he'd invited into his box. Mina squinted through the flickering shadows, recognizing a widowed countess the gossip rags loved to spill ink over. He wasn't altering his ways. Mina's temper simmered before she remembered she'd been debating whether to marry a duke seconds prior.

Hell's bells. She slumped back with a huff.

The performance continued, the man at her side grinning, but she saw little aside from the gorgeous rat across the theatre.

He'd cut his hair. The most stylish she'd ever seen it. Dressed in formal black and gray, he served up a feast for the famished gazes in the theatre, hers included.

She let her opera glasses fall to her lap, stung by sorrow. Griff had drifted back into his life like she was never there. Returned to his business in Shoreditch—this she'd read in *About Town* last week. Placed another tart on his arm. Another opera. Another ball. There'd been no transformation for him, their encounter in the closet a passing fancy.

Apparently, undone was a fleeting state for rakes.

Mina feigned a coughing fit and gave Langston a gentle nudge. "May I?" she asked, gesturing to the aisle.

He jumped to his feet, bowing, a lock of ashen hair dropping across his forehead. That he should annoy her after how gracious he'd been, proved how ill-mannered *she* was. But you couldn't remove the racetrack from the girl, even with costly clothing and refined-through-much-practice comportment. "Allow me to escort you," he whispered near her ear. Close enough to tell her she was unaffected by his presence.

She patted his arm to hold him in place. "Stay. Your sister and her companion are at the top of the stairs, and the ladies' parlor is only two doors down. We checked when we arrived. I'll be back in seconds."

His lips parted in a ready argument. Ladies didn't wander opera houses without an escort. Duchesses certainly never, *ever* did.

She left the box, ignoring his sister's pungent stare. It might be a good time for the siblings to discuss a racetrack heiress's appropriateness before any offers were made. Even if she was seeking a husband, Mina had no intention of being managed like a mindless society miss.

Since the opera was in the first act, the hallway was deserted. A candlelit wash of emerald and amber. Her slippers sank into plush carpeting as she passed the brocade settees situated randomly along the passage. Beeswax and linseed oil mixed pleasantly with lemon verbena and bergamot. Halting in an alcove to study a painting of a singer dressed in a scandalous costume, she wondered if this is what a bordello looked like—on a less sedate scale.

Mina felt him, *sensed* him before Griff drifted in beside her. She drew a covert breath. He smelled differently than he had in her flat, a peppery fragrance to accompany the new haircut. She burned to ask if his countess had anything to do with the shift.

He gestured to the painting, taking a languid sip from his flute. "Katerina Del Mónaco. A stage name, a fake accent, although her French is respectable. I believe she's actually from Surrey."

Mina snorted softly. "I'm sure you're acquainted."

His gaze shifted to her, then back to Katerina. "You believe too much of what you read in those damned newspapers, Willie."

Mina pressed her lips together, her jaw aching. He had to use that nickname and make her heart skip a beat. "How's your countess?"

"How's your duke?" he promptly returned, tossing back his champagne.

She turned to him, prepared to battle. "Aren't you missing the opera?"

Rocking on his heels, he tunneled his hand through his hair, leaving the freshly shorn strands in adorable confusion. Candlelight called out amber highlights she didn't think she'd noticed before and was vexed she was being shown now. "German librettos are a tad severe for my taste if you must know. I prefer Italian comedies."

"I quite like it," she said when she'd only been to one opera in her life, *this* one.

He grunted, his gaze fixed on the painting.

"Why attend if you don't care for Mozart, my lord?"

He pinched the bridge of his nose, exhaling through his teeth. "Because someone at White's mentioned the Duke of Langston was bringing the rookery chit he's courting. So here I am. Like a hound after a tasty bone."

His admission brought anguish as well as a dull rush of pleasure. She realized the *ton* was talking about her unsuitability, which mortified her, but Griff had come anyway. Mina trailed the toe of her slipper over a silver thread in the rug, searching her mind for what she'd admit to if they were being honest.

I miss you. I want you. My feelings scare me.

Mrs. Dove-Lyon was right about us.

Instead, true to her legacy, she blurted the worst possible thing. "This seems what a fancy bordello would look like. A treasure of velvet, every inch of trim done in gold. Without sexual congress, that is."

Griff flinched, his empty flute tumbling to the carpet. Thankfully, it didn't shatter. Going to his haunches to retrieve it, he gazed up at her, his eyes a dusky, twilight blue in the shadows. "Are you trying to give me an apoplexy in the middle of *The Magic Flute*? Carted out as the opera is halted mid-aria? Everything but my erection wilting?"

She shrugged, her cheeks flushing. "I've always wondered."

Shaking his shoulders out like he'd run a race, he shoved to his feet. "There's a fairly respectable set-up in Bloomsbury reserved for mistresses and the occasional wife of very progressive couples. The Rabbit's Lair. Masks are provided, no questions asked, a confidential endeavor. People watch, no touching allowed, so it's not as indecent as it could be. Like opera but more…" His gaze hit her, fiery hot, before shifting away. "Just more."

"Take me there."

Griff tapped the flute against his hip, drawing her eye. She let desire regulate her gaze, thoroughly studying his form. He was the tallest man in most parlors. Broad of shoulder, lean of hip, muscular where it counted but no place it didn't. The perfect balance of sinewy brawn. To her mind, he had the most impressive physique in England.

Because she was trying to be a *lady*, she wouldn't mention the wondrous part of him making a statement at the front of his trousers.

"Go back to your duke, sweet. Your gaze is lighting a fire inside me. I need a moment to put the flames out before I return to the façade. No one in that rented box inspires anything close. Too, I'm now imagining taking you to a disorderly house you shouldn't even know exists."

Mina rested against the alcove's curved wall, hands clasped before her, a guileless pose when her mind was whirling with possibilities. How to continue an association when the man desired you but didn't want to desire you? How to get a scalawag to escort you to an indecorous hovel?

She tried a different tack. "I received another query from Mr. McGowen. He was thrilled with my investigatory work. The new project involves a French count's country party and a rare vase. I'm to play the pitiable spinster cousin of a dowager aunt or some such. No one will know me, nor I them, so it's safe."

He dropped his negligent stance like a sack, straightening to tower over her. A threatening pose when she wasn't threatened. "You tell him no, Willie. You're finished with thugs as clients. Finished stealing artifacts. My returning that bloody Rembrandt was your out. Time for you to return to your beloved arithmetic."

She lifted a slim shoulder in her own show of negligence. "I already told him yes. I leave on Tuesday for Derbyshire. I simply have to make a note of the mark on the bottom of the piece. There's no theft required." She smiled when she felt like sneering. "Like the last task, until you got into it and shoved me into that blasted closet."

Making me want things I shouldn't.

Turning to a gilt-edged bamboo table, Griff popped his glass atop it. "I feel like I've been tossed into a ring, halfway into a bout I had no idea I entered. Is this a negotiation of some sort? Please tell me if it is."

Mina flicked fluff from her sleeve, undeterred by his crossness as Mozart's singspiel rolled over her in a thundering wave.

Because she'd decided.

She didn't want the Duke of Langston's lackluster grins, a thousand evenings spent with his senseless sister who disapproved of her. A family she'd never be worthy of, to her mind *or* theirs. She wanted Griffin Alastair Beckett, the irascible Viscount Kent. She wanted his moods, his wit, his intelligence. The generous heart he hid so mercilessly. The anguish he exposed to so few.

She wished to give him what he'd been missing, what they'd both been missing. Family. Love. *Companionship.*

Mrs. Dove-Lyon had known precisely what she was about, the shrewd creature.

Mina peeked at Griff as he made a slow turn of the alcove, muttering beneath his breath. He was so dazzling he made her chest ache. Why couldn't Mina secure this splendidly annoyed, wickedly cunning scoundrel if she wanted him? A man who'd keep her interested. Aroused. On her toes. A man who made her laugh, who challenged her as no other had? She'd been waiting for something as extraordinary as Griffin Beckett to happen.

She would be good for him. Deep in her determined heart, she recognized this, even if he didn't.

Her silent pledge sealed the deal.

Mina dusted her slipper along a crooked azure thread in the rug. "I'm willing to negotiate."

He knocked his knuckle on the side table, rattling the flute he'd placed atop it. "I bet you are."

"I'll ensure you and the blade in your boot receive an invitation to the country party, where you can keep an eye on the proceedings but *not* interfere in them if you, in turn, take me to Bloomsbury."

Halting, he scrubbed his hand over the back of his neck, his shorter haircut allowing a slice-of-skin view above his crisp collar. She wanted to press her lips there, then to the pulse tapping a drumbeat beneath his ear. Shifting to ease the ache slowly filling the tender area between her thighs, she comprehended what would happen if they went to Bloomsbury.

"You're too inexperienced for that style of entertainment," he whispered.

"I'm only two years younger." She had a roundabout idea of his age. "Maybe not even."

He shook his head, adjusting himself while he faced away from her. He was reacting to the idea in a similar, aroused fashion. "Age has nothing to do with it, sweet."

"Ten minutes. You can time it on that fancy Bainbridge in your pocket."

He laughed into his fist, turning to her with a flourish. "That's eight minutes longer than I need to drag you into the nearest closet." Scowling, he gestured wildly, almost pleading. "Look how that turned out."

"I thought it turned out well."

His gaze flashed, his eyes turning a molten, sizzling blue. His chest rose and fell with his exhalation. *"No,* Willie."

She passed him on her way to the duke's box, making her last attempt. "If Langston asks, I'm going to accept. Unless you see a way to stop that from happening, keep me in reserve for your beloved aunt's next proposition. Mrs. Dove-Lyon assures me she can secure other keenly desperate men."

Griff swore, his fingers circling her wrist and yanking her to a stop beside him. "You fight dirty, Wilhelmina Wright. I'll give you that. Almost dirty enough to earn the privilege to live in that rookery flat of yours."

"I fight like a chit raised around horses and men."

"We're playing with fire, sweet, you must know that. I sure as hell do. I'm fascinated, and you're curious, the most dangerous pair imaginable." His hand tensed around her wrist, drawing her a step closer. The flecks of gold in his eyes glittered like stars. "I feel singed from your gaze. Let alone what I'd feel if I put my hands on you."

His gloved hold burned through the sleeve of her gown, warming her to her toes. "I thought you liked to roll the dice, Kent. Isn't that what you told me? And that Langston wasn't suited for the wager. Consider this a dare, if that makes it more edible, a confection you wish to eat before anyone else does."

He growled low in his throat, and with a sharp glance down the corridor, pulled her from the alcove. He guided her to a narrow staircase at the back and took them to a darkened hallway crowded with pushcarts and boxes. A space for theater staff, not those attending performances.

Vexed, she shook free of his grasp. Because of his amorous activities with thespians, the scoundrel knew the layout of the building. Her heart lodged in her throat as she imagined what he'd done down here—and with whom.

Halting before a crimson door marked *Attire,* Griff jiggled the knob, finding it unlocked. He was inside in a flash, returning with a black cloak that was obviously part of an actor's costume. Tossing it over her shoulders, he arranged the hood until he was the only person in England who would recognize a racetrack urchin peeking from beneath the velvet folds.

Anger in his actions, he cradled her face in his broad palms and backed her against the doorjamb. Trapped her with his long body if she thought to get away, when she had no intention of fleeing. Her lips opened, inviting. *Yes.* Her tongue engaging his in the dance she'd found he adored, nothing tender about it.

The man lived as he kissed, on the edge.

The embrace was a promise—and a threat. Passion unleashed in a surprising flood of emotion from a man society deemed a dispassionate soul. When Mina knew Griffin Beckett felt deeply. Would *love* deeply, given the chance. She verified her belief in the furious beat of his heart, the flutter of his pulse where his wrist grazed her jaw, the ragged moan leaving his lips to travel over hers, his tenderness despite his yearning.

He didn't push as hard or as far as he could—because she would have agreed to everything.

"Why are you stopping?" she whispered when he drew a hairsbreadth away.

"I could kiss you until the end of time, Willie. If I weren't so busy saving you from one disaster after another." He nipped her jaw, his hand snaking beneath the cloak's hood to cup her nape, tilting her gaze to his starbright one. "I've never experienced such a thing, where I'm confused about my end and another's beginning. Where this supposedly simple piece is so bloody good that I'm scared, to my studs, of the next. No woman has ever brought me to a coward's precipice. Not here." He laughed, sending a champagned breath across her cheek. "I'm not sure I like it."

Stomping footfalls on the floor above brought them staggering apart.

He braced his arm on the wall, blocking her. "I have my own deal to propose, sweet. Your agreement before I have a servant deliver a note to your duke saying Miss Wright had to leave abruptly due to a fainting spell."

"I've never fainted in my life, not once. And he's not *my* duke."

"Not unless you deny him." He grunted, his smile beautiful and merciless. "This is my offer. Rules in place, parties in complete accord. One, I agree to your requested ten minutes in the Lair. Not eleven. *Ten.* Two, you secure my invitation to your country party, a fete I have suspicions about the suitability of, but that's another story. Three, we record the mark on the bottom of the vase, deed done, then return to London. You to your crooked books and simpering dukes, me to my business ventures and that damned viscountcy."

"And your countesses. Don't forget those eager chits in need of lots and lots of attention."

His jaw flexed, his lips tightening. "Agreed, Willie?"

"Agreed, my lord," Mina whispered and adjusted her hood over her face seconds before a troop of actors flooded the hallway. One woman, dressed as a milkmaid, winked at Griff as she passed.

"Did you see that?" Mina swatted his shoulder. It was rock hard and layered in muscle, flexing beneath her touch. "Quit laughing, you scoundrel!"

"I am a scoundrel. And you should be scared, sweet, because you're mine for every one of those ten minutes."

Grasping her hand, he went in search of someone to alert a duke to the sudden departure of an heiress.

CHAPTER SEVEN

Where a viscount spends twelve minutes in paradise

T HE RABBIT'S LAIR was better—and worse—than Griff remembered.

Better because the establishment maintained an atmosphere of discretion for the ladies in attendance. Masks, cloaks, even a chit he could have sworn was wearing a wig. Glasses of champagne resting on silver slavers, the scent of gardenias and roses from the bouquets scattered about riding the air. Velvet and brocade settees and sofas, not a stain to be found, which wouldn't have been the case in an East End bawdy house. Covert smiles and polite laughter, a genuine effort to not stare at anyone, lest you recognize or be recognized.

A façade of graciousness in a den of iniquity.

Worse because the moment he'd escorted Willie into the paneled foyer and down the lavish hallway, warring instincts took hold and yanked like he'd been placed on a rack. Protectiveness, desire, fondness, and a thrumming tinge of fury. He *liked* this woman. A lot. In a friendship way…but with shades of something more profound.

It was senseless, but he wanted to show her the world, even this rather lewd slice.

He wanted to see her bloom like one of the roses on the Lair's mantel, and this was an urge he'd not been able to conquer. Not at King's Theatre, where he'd scribbled a note to a duke, signed a name that wasn't his—an elderly gentleman of excellent standing who hadn't been in attendance but could've been. That kind gent could have seen Willie stumble on the stairs, then he and his baroness escort her home when she felt unwell.

It was a probable lie, the best kind to make. He only hoped Langston wasn't so smitten he'd check on Willie on the way to his ducal manse. They'd have to untangle that mess later if he did.

Rolling his shoulders, Griff reclined against the veranda's open door, ready to flee. Willie stood fidgeting by his side, her flute disappearing inside that ridiculous hooded cloak at too-swift intervals. She would be foxed before her ten minutes were up, corrupted in a way he wished he didn't want to see—when the utter truth was, he did.

He checked his pocket watch. Six minutes remaining.

He'd allotted ten because sensual sport at the Rabbit's Lair had a regimented tempo. The couple arrived, kissed, fondled, undressing slowly, giving those who'd only wished to see this early bit of titillation the ability to leave. Griff figured five minutes, if that's what they had left once the entertainment arrived, should have them exiting about the moment the situation got interesting.

Too interesting for him to observe with a woman he desired more than any on this planet.

"Five minutes," he whispered near her cloaked ear after another check of the time.

She waved her flute, irritated by his persistence in sticking to the rules. Well, that was too damned bad. He wasn't going to debauch her or bloody ruin himself in the soul sense, not in this room, anyway. Even with her mask, with no one knowing who she was, *he* knew. The fact that he suspected—concerned wasn't stating it too bluntly—his heart might be involved with this stubborn chit made him unsure about the entire mess.

Unsure about letting Willie see this debacle when it was her right to see it. To be curious, to yearn, as he did. He didn't own her, after all.

Although he wasn't sure about letting her marry Langston.

Or about letting her marry anyone but him.

He'd agreed to wed her, hadn't he? Griff gave his almost-wife a peeking side-glance, dismayed when his chest constricted in a manner that felt, well, treacherous. He opened his mouth, set to tell her they needed to leave when the entertainment strolled into the room through the hallway door. The chit was buxom and blond, the man muscular, dark, with a footman's build. They wore masks and clothing that looked ordinary but involved fewer layers, a fact the occupants of the parlor would see once the disrobing began.

They started kissing straightaway, arms winding around each other. It wasn't a kiss as hot as his and Willie's, it wasn't *real*...but it was enough to get the ball rolling. Observing, Willie backed into the door, her breath leaving her in a wispy rush that held him pinned in place.

Griff had forgotten this sensation if he'd ever truly experienced it.

Arousal not by sight but by *feel*. In the mind more than the body. The couple across from him, agreed, they were enticing and going to do wicked things to each other, but the woman next to him, her slim fingers clasped around her flute, her lips—merely the rounded bow, all he could see beneath the hood—parted slightly, her tongue sliding out to moisten the bottom, *she* was the key to his longing.

A bloody frightening thought.

Shifting to hide his burgeoning erection, he checked his Bainbridge watch. Four minutes.

Touching the players was not allowed, and the Lair's heavies cir-cled the room, fists clenched, urging the crowd of twenty or so back a step. Griff moved in front of Willie, not enough to cut her view but sufficient to announce possession.

Her body was a welcome presence, her breasts hitting him just below his shoulder blades. She wedged her cheek against his bicep, peeking around him, leaning into him. Closing his eyes, he took in the sound of her faint breaths and the scent of jasmine, the gentle knock of tree limbs against each other in the courtyard. The call of a nightingale. The crackle of the hearth fire.

When he opened them, they had one minute left. The couple were impishly working on fastenings, buttons, and ties, all part of the show. The brute's shirt was parted, revealing a muscular chest and flat belly. Willie's fingers clasped his forearm, and Griff promptly lost his thought. Agitated, he stood a bit straighter. He had an excellent physique from twice-weekly fencing matches and the occasional boxing club visit.

Despite his discomfiture, he generously let Willie have an additional two minutes, for a total of twelve.

Because she was resting against him so sweetly, so trustingly. He'd not had many people in his life trust him. Besides, the couple was working at a leisurely pace, her bodice parted, his shirt floating to the floor, still not much more than one would witness at Covent Garden. Hands, however, were beginning to wander, the participants responding in a sincere fashion.

When they began to simulate the act in a grinding rhythm, layers of clothing not enough to hide the implication, Griff turned and took Willie's hand, shielding her view. She was wide-eyed, her cheeks flushed, her mask askew. Her chest rose with rapid exhalations, those breasts he wanted to lick every inch of surging against the rounded neck of her gown. Affected, provoked, as he was.

Had he expected less? That he recognized the passion buried beneath her surface made the situation lethal.

When she mouthed one word—*carriage*—he decided he was a goner.

So was she. As there was only so much temptation a man could take.

They were down the veranda's staircase and traversing the misty mews at the rear of the manse in seconds. His carriage was parked on Great Russell Street, a hulking beast of a conveyance that had belonged to his father. He waved off the coachman as they approached, hoisting Willie into the interior and climbing in behind her without a clue what he was doing.

She surprised him when he shouldn't be surprised by anything she did, by fastening her lips to his before he could utter a word, nailing him to the velvet squabs.

Jolting, the carriage bounced over cobblestones, and she tumbled into his lap.

Circling her waist, he brought her against his chest, unable to think anything but *finally, yes.* She wiggled free of the cloak, lips parting, tongue caressing his, controlling the pace. She'd learned quickly what he liked, what set him aflame. Teasing strokes, then absolute abandon. Breathless, aching passion. A kiss to fall into and die inside of. Gladly.

His hands were full of her, his mind clouded. How to deny her or himself when they were this good together? Her skirt was easily dragged to her waist, his fingers curled around her hip, drawing her into the sensual dance they'd witnessed in the Lair's parlor before he remembered himself.

Remembered *where* they were.

Pushing her away, he settled her brow on his shoulder and gasped into her hair. His cock was in a rather distressed position against his trouser buttons, his body tense with need. "Not here. Not the first time, in any case."

She sighed, longing clear in the quiver of her body. He desired to pleasure her in that moment to the heavens and back. Why his bloody feelings had to get involved, he wished he knew. They never had before.

"You and your blasted rules, Griffin Beckett."

"You mean more to me than..."—he swallowed, gestured to nothing she could see crushed against him like a flower between pages—"...than this."

Catching the pained note in his voice, she drew back. Her eyes were glowing lavender orbs in the muted moonlight, unfathomably beautiful. Like the woman. Wit, intellect, determination. He'd abandoned a perfect package on that damned altar. "You're saying yes, just not here?"

"You'll be ruined," he pointed out, unable not to. "Once you've experienced pleasure of this sort, you find yourself thinking of little else. I'm warning you."

She laughed, delighted, dogged to the core. "Why can't we say I'll be enlightened? Better prepared for marriage, even. Worldly. Free. *Knowing.*"

He let out a tight exhalation, not thrilled with any of those options.

She trailed her fingertip across his bottom lip. "Don't be cross. I want this night. I want *you.* Let me choose. Take the burden off those broad shoulders of yours."

"I loathe this carriage. My last conversation with my father was in this thing," he admitted, disbelieving, even as the confession slipped from his lips, that he was telling her this. "A vile argument, truth be told. He died a fortnight later, and a troubled viscount was born."

"Ah," she said, understanding, and possibly, she sincerely did. Sitting back enough to let him draw a full breath, she placed her hand on his chest, too near his heart for comfort. "You weren't close, then?"

"We weren't anything. My mother, even less. She didn't care for children, especially her own. All 'jam stains and drool' were the first words I recall from her. I think I was happier in school, away from them. And they gave me no choice about that."

Willie rose on shaky legs, shook her skirt and settled on the seat across from him. "You're trying to divert my attention to other topics.

Give me a chance to rethink my decision."

He nodded, his gaze helplessly tracking her every move. "Is it working?"

She grinned, already wise in ways, although she might not be aware of it. "Not a bit. I'm merely giving *you* time to calm down before we dive back in. In whatever bedchamber we land in, yours or mine."

He didn't argue, instead glanced out the window, the midnight streets of London passing at remarkable speed. The occasional cart and drunken wanderer dotting the lane, flashes of color when all the richness in the world sat across from him. "We could follow the initial agreement. The contracts are in my study drawer, still crisp as a new pound note." When she failed to respond, he looked to find her tracing a rip in the velvet cushion. "I mean marriage, sweet."

She laughed, a hiccupping sound that charmed his stockings off. "This is mad, and not to use your words, though I will, but you've come to mean more to me than that."

Miserably, he understood. They weren't going to play the game of pretending to care when they were actually starting to care. They were trapped in the unhappy middle, or at least he was.

Unable to fully define what he felt—and pressed to define it or let the girl go.

While he sat there stewing, compiling a list of pros and cons and wondering what Willie Wright felt for *him* because she'd never said it, she moved to sit next to him, cradled his face in her palms and pulled him into the gentlest kiss of his life.

There was no denying her then.

CHAPTER EIGHT

Where an independent woman admits to wanting everything

A MAN'S HOME held secrets.

Revealed things he wouldn't.

As with most of life, the answers lay scattered amongst the details.

Mina took in as many as she could—books stacked in a darkened corner, scraps of paper on the bedside table, overturned Hoby boots by the hearth, a stray stocking beneath the settee—as Griff closed his bedchamber door and leaned against it, his expression seven shades of wicked. The space smelled of him, spicy and male. He made no move to reach her, merely began to unfurl his cravat with sure, determined tugs, his gaze doing a sluggish sweep of her body, lingering at her waist, her breasts, before rising to her face.

She felt the examination like she would his touch, her skin warming, her heartbeat unsteady. Wrapping her arm around the bedpost, she leaned into it. She was winded from the race they'd taken up the back staircase, narrow and dim and meant for servants, fleeing whoever the viscount in residence thought might see them at this late hour.

He wished to protect her from risks she was willing to take.

He'd stopped to kiss her—*twice*, pressing her into the wall, then the railing at the top of the stairs—adding mightily to her breathlessness.

She rather hoped he continued to undress and let her look her fill.

He halted, the strip of silk gliding through his fingers and dropping in a wisp to the floor. Without another word, he toed off his boots, then began to work on his boned shirt buttons, exposing a swath of olive skin and dark chest hair. "You don't have an ounce of fear thrumming through your delectable body, sweet, while I'm debating what the bloody hell I'm doing. Although it's not fear running through me, either."

Her stomach clenched. "You don't want me?"

He paused, startled, his fingers falling from his shirt. A task she'd be happy to complete for him if he dared come closer. Shaking his head, laughing softly, he crossed to her in a resolute stride.

"Does this feel like a man who doesn't want you?" he asked and pressed her hand over his rigid shaft in the boldest move he'd ever made with her. Instinctively, she curled her fingers around him as he groaned, his lids fluttering. Finally, he was treating her as a woman and not a teacup he worried about crushing if he held it too tightly. "I want your lips circling me, your teeth sinking into my skin, your body surrounding me. I'm greedy and voracious. Blind with hunger. Confused by it. Does that properly address your concerns?"

"Voracious," Mina whispered, heat lodging between her thighs as he stared at her lips forming the word, a fierce look seizing his features.

Stepping in, he cupped her cheek, capturing her gaze, then her mouth.

"*Now*," was all he said before he took her under.

Between navigating ties, hooks, buttons, they kissed, the bedpost providing a steadying presence. Wiggling free of layers that dropped with their inhibitions. Amazingly, amusement was involved when she ripped his shirtsleeve in her eagerness as he fumbled with the hooks at the back of her gown, not as proficient as she'd expected.

At least with her, he wasn't.

She traced the still-rough edges of the scar beneath his ribs with the gentlest touch possible, thinking that someday soon, she'd press her lips there and slide lower.

When she was down to her chemise and he down to his drawers, he backed her into the bed and with a teasing growl, pushed her to the mattress. Flipping her hair from her face, she went to her elbow with a snort of laughter. Towering over her, his gaze roved the length of her. With a force of will and a dash of courage she didn't know she had, she let him look. Pebbled nipples pressing against silk, the dark swath of hair between her legs visible, *oh, so* visible, she was undoubtedly a sight.

He scrubbed his hand across his chin, down his chest, halting before he touched himself. Though his arousal was tenting his drawers in an unspeakably affecting way. "*Ah*, sweet, you're so beautiful. I don't know if I deserve you. Deserve this."

Mina pinched the waist of her chemise between her fingers and lifted it above her knees, stopping when the hem hit her lower thighs. "Am I going to have to convince you, Griffin Alastair Beckett?"

Bewildered, his gaze sought hers. His eyes were a blazing, stormy-sea blue. "You've been kissed before, am I right?" He palmed his belly, a scowl twisting his lips. "I find myself becoming angry thinking about this, which I realize is hypocritical. Yet, I can't help myself."

She smothered her amusement, recalling the fragility of men. "There were two grooms at Wright's, and I received a kiss from each." Tilting her head, she held up a finger. "Actually, two from the one...I think his name was Samuel. Nothing like the kisses I've shared with you, but to my lonely mind, they were better than nothing."

"Off," he murmured, gesturing to her chemise.

"Off," she murmured, gesturing to his drawers.

They followed each other's command, staring soundlessly when the deed was done.

His body was glorious. Lean and long, and as she'd noted previously, muscular only where necessary for perfect symmetry. Shoulders, biceps. A wealth of hair between his nipples trailed to his flat belly. Her breath caught in her throat. His shaft...*oh*, she wasn't sure about that.

"It will fit, I promise," he whispered and grazed his calloused fingertip along the pad of her foot, circling her ankle, calf, knee, thigh. Then he was climbing atop her, rocking the bed while she struggled to control her pulse, his hand diving into her hair and drawing her into his kiss before she could reason this out.

She lost focus, desire taking hold, her caresses chasing his. His weight settling over her was an unfamiliar delight, one she welcomed. A last glance, the lone lamp's glow lighting his beauty before logic dissolved.

His hips pressed her thighs apart, where they rocked, sinking into each other. He was hard, she soft, slick heat joining their bodies. A hearth fire started in her belly and flared, warming her from head to toe. Griff left the kiss, lips trailing her jaw, her throat, finally lowering to her breasts. His groans were muffled against her nipple, the tight bud drawn between his teeth, his tongue circling. Moving from one to the other until she cried out and twisted into his touch.

This sound encouraged his exploration without another legible word spoken.

His hand journeyed between their bodies, finding her ready, eager. Her hips rose, sending his finger inside her in a determined push. Her fist clenched in the counterpane, her back arching as he began to slowly thrust. His ownership made her tremble, bringing her pleasure close.

"That's it," he said into the plump swell of her breast as he stroked in a measured cadence set to drive her mad. "Take what I'm offering. Be greedy."

The adventure wasn't hers to manage after that.

She merely followed, instinct guiding passion guiding desire as his lazy murmurs rippled over her. Sweat broke out over his body, over hers. Her nails dug into his shoulder blades, into his hip, urging him into a dance she was only beginning to understand.

"Come for me, sweet," he whispered, his lips dipping into the hollow at the base of her throat and licking. "This might help." Then, he pressed his thumb to the swollen bud at the top of her sex, circling, circling, sending her over the edge.

He swallowed her cries, the kiss spiraling. She clung to him, body braced, ripples of bliss rolling like waves through her. Only when she'd begun to calm did he position himself into place at her entrance.

She opened her eyes to find his gaze fixed on her. Blue, so blue, scorching.

Shifting, she reached for him, gratified by his groan when her fingers circled his shaft. He was sleek, hard, smooth. She tested his weight, his length, learning how to touch him. "I think I'm going to like this."

He captured her hand and pressed it into the mattress. "You're going to love it." He shouldered a bead of sweat from his jaw and angled his hips, edging his cock inside her. "You've a talent, Willie, unknown to anyone but me."

She started to say more, joke with him about—

When he moved more forcefully, more than edging this time. Sinking, occupying, *filling*. "Griff," she sighed, the pinch of pain registering, the feeling of being stretched beyond her limit gripping her.

Reading her pleasure, he didn't cease, his movements gentle but persistent. His arm tunneled beneath her, lifting her into his shallow thrusts. "This," he whispered, adjusting her bent leg alongside his hip, "makes it easier. I'll go as slowly as you need, but for God's sake, let me in. Even if it takes all night."

Allowing her body to lose the tense hold she'd had on it, he began to thrust, cresting and falling, plunging and diving. Once they caught each other's rhythm, they moved like a wave undulating across the sea, until there wasn't an end or beginning but merely two souls working as one.

The seconds merged and time suspended. His hand lingered on at her waist. Hips bumping, lips meeting, then parting and meeting again. Her nipples abraded by the hair on his chest until they ached. Her core open for him, to him. Near the end, when her body had caught fire again, when he'd begun touching her, adding another element to the dance, she found herself clutching him, shoulders, forearms, guiding the tempo.

Her legs circled his waist, this elemental move one he moaned in ecstasy over. The bedframe creaked with his strokes, the sound mixed with their labored breaths and the tick of a clock in the room.

She wished to expire from pleasure—and was profoundly glad when it seized her.

He recorded her fall, his eyes hot, his skin slick, his breath labored against her throat. He followed soon after, his hand grasping the headboard for purchase as he left being a gentleman behind.

It was fury, passionate fury and nothing but. Moaning, gasping desire.

Pulling from her body, Griff spent away from her. Understandable protection, but her heart shuddered as he experienced his release without her.

There were no words, mere breathing a struggle. The air in the bedchamber compressed, hot and thick.

Falling to his back, he tucked her into his side, in a hidden nook she found she fit quite well. His lips grazed the crown of her head, her temple, his arm locking and holding. His heartbeat raced beneath her breast in wild abandon, his chest rising and falling as he sought to recover.

At that moment, they were equals. She'd destroyed him as he'd destroyed her.

This is trouble, she thought as slumber overcame her.

And trouble felt a lot like love.

CHAPTER NINE

Where a viscount admits to fear and loathing

IF THIS WAS love, Griff didn't want anything to do with it.

Willie lounged on the terrace stairs leading to his estate's over-grown garden, clutching an apple in her fist, humming a jaunty tune as she chewed. Her hair would take two to untangle, and her gown was utterly beyond repair. Anyone who looked at her flushed cheeks, the sluggish smile on her face, those wiggling toes, would deduce the master of the house had tupped his guest not once but *twice*. (As well as other lewd activities eventually making a wreck of his chamber.)

His massive medieval bed, antique escritoire and the Aubusson rug before his hearth had never experienced such exquisite abuse.

Dawn was leaking across the horizon in a rolling ginger burst, and here he sat, a beetle in amber, transfixed by the sight of his almost-wife's sedate bliss. She hadn't let him do more than tend to her, as well as he could with a scrap of linen and the chilled water in his basin before dragging him, radiantly pleased, down the back staircase and out of the doors.

He'd never stayed with a chit after tupping, much less laughed during. Talked in between sharing bites of fruit as a dense London mist swirled about them. Why, he'd rarely visited the pond at the back of his property, not since he was a lad, much less circled it in bare feet and weak knees, grass tickling his ankles.

This morning felt unusual. Enchanting. He wasn't a man plagued by compulsions, needing to sleep next to the same person every night. It was unfathomable. Silly.

Tremors unrelated to sexual congress pulsed through him in tiny, terror-filled quivers.

Because love had never been part of the bargain.

Any bargain.

With a shrewd smile, Willie offered him the apple, the second she'd consumed. Blowing out a breath, he tugged on his trousers and perched beside her on the top step, realizing his half-stance appeared as if he was preparing to flee. It was only that he'd never seen a woman respond so gleefully to his carnal consideration, even as he had a reputation for delivering the goods.

Well, he'd wanted to see her blossom, hadn't he? Keeping his hands where they should be was enough of a challenge, tucked in his pockets and away from Willie Wright. There was no need to wipe the dab of ink from their encounter on the desk, from her cheek.

She took another bite of the apple, chewing slowly. "Your gardens are in dismal shape, but the house is gorgeous. Honestly, with a little work, the rest could be as well."

He gazed into the distance, remembering climbing the hedges as a boy. Mostly hiding from his father when the earl had been in one of what his staff called a "black mood." Before he'd been banished, Griff had loved the place. Before being sent to Rugby and made to feel there wasn't any need to return, even on breaks between terms. Student housing had indeed been bleak during Christmastide. "I know the shrubs look horrid, the lawns worse. I haven't had funds, until this new venture came about, to maintain them properly. I'm meeting with my estate manager next week. I'd asked my brother, Dominic, to help manage them last year."

Griff shrugged and rested against the marble column. No need to go there. Dom had spent the estate budget at the Lyon's Den. Or that opium nest on Curzon. Griff wasn't sure, only that the blunt had left his desk's cash box and never returned.

"You're good at taking care of people."

He turned his head, checking to see if she was joking. "I don't think," he started, then let his words fizzle out. He didn't know what to say, only wished his cheeks would cool. Viscounts didn't *blush*.

She gestured with the fruit, munching softly. "I was lonely, too. My mother died, and my father wasn't a father, unlike the blokes you see on the street, carrying their children around on their backs and tossing them balls and such. But we had a home and food on the table. Wood in the hearth. How's a person to complain about receiving no affection when there's such misery in the world? Who cares about love when there's starvation?"

A low ache spiraled in his chest and spread to his throat, fairly choking him. He'd never talked to anyone about his childhood, even his siblings. They were younger, frivolous beings he supposed he *was* taking care of.

To them, he was merely the boy who'd become the earl.

"What about the rest of this? That piece you mentioned after we tumbled off the bed?" Her gaze shifted to him in a side-eyed bit of flirtation.

He wasn't fooled—or immune. His cock shifted, coming to life.

"I shouldn't have mentioned that," he said and reached for the apple, taking a neat bite instead of offering more suggestions. Although the image of his head between her legs, licking, sucking, his tongue thrusting, wasn't leaving him. And the other, her mouth on *him*. The opportunity was there to do more unless he tossed her into his carriage and sent her home.

Because they hadn't gotten there yet didn't mean they wouldn't.

Willie dusted her toes through a pile of leaves on the stair. "I think I'd like that after seeing how good you are at—"

He was beside her immediately, hand covering her mouth. "You're killing me, sweet. We already went too far, carried this past what we'd agreed to. Which wasn't half-naked confessions while eating fruit on my veranda at dawn."

She snatched the apple back and plunked the half-eaten core into the azalea bush by her side. "I don't know why you're cross. The other things we could do was your idea. 'Another avenue of pleasure,' isn't that how you put it?"

Squatting, Griff rocked back on his heels and drummed his thumb on his knee. It was time to introduce the controversial subject circling his mind. "I want you to cancel the vase mission. Tell Buster McGowen you'll cook his books but nothing else. No more sneaking around pretending to be an investigator or whatever it is you're doing."

Willie jerked like he'd poked her with a needle. "Oh, *ho*, you think that, do you?" She was on her feet quickly enough to illustrate how much she appreciated his advice.

He rose with a defeated sigh, figuring this was how the night would end. Badly.

She marched down the stairs, then back up while he watched, his body hungry for her. All that passion, *ah*, she'd exhibited every ounce of it last night, astride him on that bloody desk. Kneeling before him on the hearthrug. Curious, witty, sensual, confounding Wilhelmina Wright.

Her willfulness was wonderful in bed but shite to handle out of it.

She halted before him, stabbing her finger in his chest. Her eyes were a deep, dark amethyst that spelled trouble. "You think ambition is unappealing in a woman, is that it? Well, I'll tell you what's worse. Waiting for someone to save you or give your life *meaning*. Solve the puzzle for you. Men don't wait for that. They use their power to open every door available to them yet sneer when females do the same."

He tried to grasp her shoulders, but she danced out of reach. "I simply don't want you going to some demi-monde country party in the guise of stealing a bloody vase! You think Langston would marry you if that ever, *ever* got out?"

She turned to him, her gaze stricken, cheeks as ashen as the dogwood blooms scattered about.

He'd said something wrong, irretrievably wrong.

Wait. Did she want to marry him now? After he'd decided he wanted to marry her? Although decisions such as these shouldn't be made after the most rousing bout of sex in one's life. He'd resolved to take a week to gather the necessary paperwork, to let his body—and hers—settle before he asked.

But he'd been damned set on asking.

"Willie," Griff called as she stalked across the lawn, breasts bobbing, hips swinging, heading to the stables on the property's western edge. If she thought he was letting her ride one of his mounts home, bare feet and bouncing bosom, she didn't know him well.

He took care of the people he loved, didn't she recall?

She was in tears when he reached her, bowed against the side of that fucking carriage he hated. Great, gasping sobs he'd not imagined a girl like her would suffer from. The horses had begun to whinny in their stalls in commiseration.

He froze beside her, stunned, his heart squeezing until he thought *he* might cry. He reached but paused before he touched her. "Whatever I said, I didn't mean. Not in the way you're taking it. I'm still fuzzy in my head after that little trick you did with your teeth." He searched for a handkerchief, but he was wearing only rumpled trousers and a hastily misbuttoned shirt.

They were a sight to behold, both of them.

She sniffled into her sleeve, adding further ruin to a gown ready for the rubbish bin. "You'd let Langston have me if he asked. Duchess Wilhelmina, at your service. I'm merely like all the others to you." She laughed, a dire edge to the sound.

It was a terrible time to realize that she was the most gorgeous creature in England and that he'd never desire anyone, mind and body, the way he desired her. "Willie, stop. Let me rephrase what I said in better terms."

"The ridiculous thing is, I thought I was *different*. Foolish, foolish chit." She leaned back against the carriage, bawling. "I'm overwrought. See what three spells of pleasure does to a person?"

He was loathe to remind her, but it had been four.

"Sweet," he started, his words stacking up on each other in his mind. *I love you. I'm not letting that ridiculous duke have you. Imagine how he is in bed if he holds a billiard cue like a child? And viscountess is quite a handy title.* "I—"

"I would like to return home, Kent." She flicked her hand in a commanding gesture without looking at him. She would have made a magnificent duchess, but he sure as hell wasn't telling her that when she was in this state. "Not *home*, home. Limehouse, if you please. Call your groom, our night has ended."

Griff flexed his jaw, hearing it pop. "You can't go anywhere dressed like that, Willie."

"Will you stop with that infernal nickname?" Searching the stable's main chamber, she strode to a line of pegs along the wall and ripped a blanket free. Tossing it over her shoulders, she clambered into the carriage without his assistance, a horsey stench drifting through the open window. Leaning out, she stared him down, her glorious eyes shining with tears and fury. "This isn't the first time you've sent a chit home in less than appropriate clothing, am I right?"

Griff stayed silent. He couldn't lie to her, he sincerely couldn't.

"My father didn't give me much, but this advice comes to mind. It's actions, *guv*, not words." Blowing out a breath, she jerked the shade down, ending any notion of him climbing in with her. "I'll wait here until your groom arrives, my lord."

Cursing, Griff stalked to the main house, guessing he had no choice but to let her go for now.

Until he figured out how to win the war. And the girl.

CHAPTER TEN

Where a viscount strategizes

B ESSIE DOVE-LYON KEPT him waiting when the invitation had been hers.

"More a command," Griff grumbled, tapping his tumbler against the damp windowpane in her study. It had been raining for two days, typical spring weather that had his mood in the gutter alongside the rubbish floating down Cleveland Row. He didn't turn when the door opened nor when the swish of his aunt's skirt sounded as she crossed the room.

Stepping beside him, she took his glass and sipped, beneath her veil, quite the trick. Her perfume was light and enticing, at odds with the hard-hitting woman wearing the fragrance. "I'll hand it to you, you wrecked the wooing. As considerable a romantic disaster as any I've witnessed, and that's saying something in my line of work."

"Have you seen her?" Griff asked, unable to stand there a second longer when his aunt might have news. It had been two weeks since Willie stormed back to Limehouse wrapped in his stinking horse blanket. In the days since she'd rejected bouquets, notes, all the ridiculous avenues a man took to apologize. In desperation, he'd even gone begging at her home but been promptly shown the door by a footman twice his size with missing teeth and a granite jaw. Probably one of Buster McGowen's bruisers sent to protect her since no one else had been slated for the job.

Actions, wasn't that what she'd wanted?

But somehow, his were the *wrong* actions.

"I have," Bessie said, returning his glass with a sigh. "Would you like to hear how that went? She's furious with me, too, for hiding our familial association. For introducing you, for letting her fall in love. As if I have any control over that. I was able to talk her out of going after that vase, however, for which you can thank me later."

Griff choked on a slug of brandy, turning to his aunt in a fluster. "She told you that? Used those words, those *exact* words?" If he had confirmation that Willie loved him, he would find her now, *today*.

Her veil quivered as she released a strangled laugh. "My dear boy, you've been brought low by Cupid's arrow. I never thought I'd live to see it. Griffin Beckett, Viscount Kent, lovesick. This would have done my dear Colonel's heart good to see."

Griff swore and drained his glass. "Don't tease me, Bessie. This undertaking is as entertaining as a rash."

"You're comparing love to the pox?"

Prowling to the sideboard, he poured another glass, telling himself this would be it for the day. He needed a moderately clear head if he wanted to figure out a way to get his almost-wife—at the very least—to talk to him. "No, being *without* her is the misery. Being with her was..." Delightful. Exhilarating. Intimate. Serene. Everything from quiet moments while reading to watching her eyes flash as he slid inside her—and all the mischief in between. "She made me happy, and the Kents aren't exactly known for happiness. She made me laugh...and that's been plenty rare, too. I know I don't deserve her, but I want her."

Greedy, aching, desperate *want*.

Bessie tunneled her hand in her skirt pocket and came out with an embroidered handkerchief. Beneath the veil, she dabbed her eyes while he watched in amazement. "I so value when love is part of the bargain. It makes everything I do worth it."

"I don't need her blunt, not a farthing," he stressed, if his intentions weren't clear. This wasn't the standard matchmaking enterprise. "This isn't about money. My venture with the Shoreditch hoodlums is going quite well, thank you. I'm finding them more ethical partners than anyone in the *ton*."

Bessie waved her handkerchief like a flag. "As a start, a piece of jewelry wouldn't be remiss."

"I have a ring I picked out after meeting her the first time." He wouldn't add that the sapphire was purplish in hue, a color close to Willie's eyes, not with his aunt on the verge of tears again. Grimacing, he tossed back the remainder of his brandy. He'd had enough weeping women lately. "This chit desires adventures, not jewels. She still wants this investigative business, and you were right, she's gotten bored handling crooked books. Unfortunately, priceless vases and stolen paintings are more her flavor."

"I heard a wild rumor about a Rembrandt."

Griff grunted. Considering the circles she traveled in, he wasn't surprised.

Bessie clicked her tongue and made a gradual circle of the study, stopping to admire a row of Wedgwood figurines on a shelf. Picking one up, she tilted it into the sconce's glow. "Help her then, in the way only a man of influence can."

Griff propped his hip on the sideboard, willing to accept advice. "Such as?"

"Besides a charming wit, a pleasing face, a generous heart and a reputation that likely taught you a few things, what else do you have to offer Miss Wright?"

Scrubbing his hand over the back of his neck, Griff shrugged. "The title. But who wants that? I certainly don't, but I'm stuck with it for life."

"She might not want the title, but she might like the *connections*. Who in this town owes you, Kent? Imagine having a supportive husband rather than one who drains you dry. A visionary who sees a bigger future than you see for yourself."

Griff rested back, cradling his tumbler in his palms, crystal facets dancing across his skin. *Hmm...* "There are a few markers I'm holding close to the vest."

Bessie replaced the curio on the shelf with a neat click. "I thought so, shrewd fellow."

"I could help her build her business. Contacts, associations. Hell, all we do at White's is talk each other to death and enter bets in that ridiculous book. Surely someone needs a discreet investigator." Griff gazed into his empty glass, the picture becoming clear. "I support her dreams to gain my own, is it?"

Bessie settled against the window ledge with what Griff imagined was a wide smile. "Go get your girl, Kent."

THE FIRST OFFER of employment, a request to locate a missing family heirloom for a marquess, was odd as Mina had gained a reputation for problem-solving among a lowbrow set. Members of the *ton* had never approached her for anything except recommendations on locating an exceptional thoroughbred. The second, from an elderly earl who wished to find a distant cousin who might be his heir, sounded alarm bells in her mind.

When a third assignment arrived from a dowager countess searching for a replica of a doll she'd cherished as a child, Mina reasoned who was behind the growth of her business. Griffin Beckett, her not-so-silent partner. The man she was frantically in love with.

A man she hadn't seen in sixteen days. Sixteen agonizing days.

And the nights? Hopeless, absolutely hopeless.

Mina tapped the calling card that had arrived this morning in a blank envelope against the tufted seat of the hack, her heart doing a slow roll in her chest. Yearning, she had learned the past weeks, was a living thing.

The card was simple. White vellum and crisp black ink.

W.L.W. Investigations
30 Wimpole Street
Marylebone, London

Was a certain wicked viscount going to be waiting for her at the end of this journey?

When the carriage slowed, Mina nudged aside the curtain and peeked out the window. The building they'd halted before was on a quiet lane of converted carriage houses, Georgian in design, a street or two from the bustling shops on High Street. The coachman moved to assist her before she could climb out—as if she were a lady in waiting.

Which she wasn't, but maybe, just maybe, she could be.

The promise of rain misted the air, curling her hair about her cheeks despite her best effort to contain it. Her gown was serviceable but not lovely. She wasn't dressed for seduction or persuasion. She was merely Wilhelmina Wright, horse heiress, mathematician, and amateur investigator, which would have to be enough.

The sidewalk before the modest dwelling was well maintained, the shutters on the lone front window a stately blue. If the shade was near the color of a certain scoundrel's eyes, Mina decided, for the moment, to ignore it. However, her breath caught when she reached the entrance, and she stumbled to a stop.

W.L.W. Investigations, the sign on the door stated in neat gold lettering.

She laughed and clutched her hands to her chest in delight. Why, her darling viscount had secured her a proper place of business—and not a rookery hideaway, either. The sign made it official! Beaming, Mina stepped back to get a better look at the place. Nothing fancy, but she found it perfect. It was a real office, not some nook she used to conceal what she was doing.

Also, none of her clients liked traveling to Shoreditch, even the hoodlums who'd grown up just down the street.

She opened the door and stepped inside, unsure of what she'd find.

The waiting area was tidy with two scuffed leather armchairs settled before a desk. The space smelled faintly of coffee and cheroots, the walls covered with paintings you forgot the moment your gaze left them. The young man behind the desk was fresh-faced, bespectacled, with the darkest hair Mina had ever seen, so black it shone blue in the lamplight's glow. His clothing was rumpled but of decent quality, the garments struggling to contain a maturing build. He glanced at her without a hint of surprise, the toothpick dangling from his mouth bobbing with his smile.

"Trying to quit the cheroots." He freed the toothpick from his teeth and gave it a twirl. "Made of bamboo, hundred to the penny. Made in the Colonies. I get 'em on the docks."

"I'm Miss Wright." She held up the card.

"Oh, aye, I've been expectin' you." Sliding two sheets across the desk, he tapped his toothpick to the top page, a dimple in his cheek flaring to life. He was a charming rascal, she'd give him that. "I have proper agreements for you to sign. Tools of the trade are being delivered tomorrow, a lock pick and opera glasses for surveillance, spying like. You have a meetin' at two with a prospective client, a dowager duchess who prefers to remain unnamed until an arrangement is reached. Crafty chit, that one. Tomorrow, blimey, who knows what catastrophe will walk through the door."

Mina forced back a snort of laughter. *Griff, what have you done?* "Lord Kent?"

The clerk jerked his thumb over his shoulder, his apple-green gaze diving back to the ledger sprawled before him. "He's puttin' up shelves in what he's calling the research room. Wanted to get it done before the duchess arrived so the place looks more finished, ready for business and all. Though, if I'm being truthful, his work is distressing. The man has talents, sure, but construction ain't one. I'll go in there and straighten 'em when he leaves for the day." He grazed the toothpick across his temple. "I have a mind for such things."

Laughing, Mina stepped inside a small office off the reception area to find Griff clutching a hammer, his gaze fixed on a shelf too crooked to hold so much as a thimble. He was dressed for work in rough cambric trousers, shirtsleeves rolled to the elbow, waistcoat flaring open, coat and cravat in a tangle on the desk at his side. His hair was in disarray as if he'd repeatedly yanked his hand through the strands during his undertaking.

A pulse of certainty pumped through her like blood. *I miss him. I love him.*

"I think it needs shoring up before you place a book on it," she whispered, trying to keep her amusement from her voice. The map of London he'd hung beside the shelf wasn't level, either.

He flinched, turning to her, the hammer tilting to tap his hip. He'd not shaved this morning, and his jaw was covered in dark stubble that mixed gloriously with his sea-blue eyes. She pressed her lips together to hide her delight. She loved when he had a slight beard, even though it wasn't fashionable, and she felt sure he'd done this for her.

She started to cross to him, but he held up the hammer, forcing her back. "Give me a moment to look at you before you touch me. Just one moment. The past two weeks have been wretched, sweet. I've barely slept, barely eaten. This love business isn't for the faint of soul, Willie. I worried the distress would break me before I got you to give me another chance."

Mina's fingers curled around the calling card, her heartbeat a loud thump in her ears, her body trembling enough for him to notice. Suddenly nervous, she swept her hand over her bodice, over the damp strands curling around her face. "Aren't you going to kiss me after that pronouncement?"

He placed the tool on the desk, his gaze making a languid sweep of her body. "If you say yes, I'll do more than kiss you. I'm going to toss you over my shoulder and carry you to the modest bedchamber I outfitted upstairs for times when we can't keep our hands off each other. Once there, I'll settle between your legs and pleasure us both to oblivion. When we stumble back down, our knees will be weak. *Weak*, I tell you. Like before, if you recall, the incident where we tumbled off my bed."

Mina's breath slipped past her lips in a ragged sigh. "Say yes to what?"

He fished a velvet box from his trouser pocket, then crooked his finger, inviting her over. His smile was patient, while the polished boot tapping the floor was not.

She hesitated, wondering when they'd stop quarreling over every little thing. Why could he not come to *her*?

"Come now, Willie, my girl. You're going to have me crawling to you many times in the future, I guarantee it. Meet me halfway, then."

Tucking the calling card she'd treasure for the rest of her life in her bodice, Mina strolled leisurely to him, letting her hips swing because he'd whispered to her once that he loved watching her cross a room. When she reached him, Griff did what he'd promised not to, pulling her into his arms, his lips seizing hers, sending reason and a stack of correspondence atop the desk flying.

They were starved for each other, the hand holding the jewelry box caught against her lower back as he tugged her closer. Hip to hip, chest to chest, they fought for fulfillment that was out of reach unless he lifted her skirt and put his hands on her. Unless she unbuttoned his trouser placket and invited him into the warm welcome of her body. As he'd warned her weeks ago, once they made love, all thoughts would lead there. Proving his statement, her mind filled with images of him poised above her, his sex stretching her, *filling* her.

Her thighs clenched, holding the wonderful feeling close. She wanted him naked and moaning that *minute*.

"Upstairs," she murmured against his neck, taking a bite and sucking.

He groaned and pressed his rigid shaft against her belly. "Willie, I want you more than I've wanted anyone. And the kicker is, I *like* you. Respect you. I think you're the cleverest woman in England. A treasure I've uncovered all on my own. I'm proud of myself for convincing you I can be good enough."

"Then let's go begin the weak-kneed wager you mentioned. Delve into my treasure box, *please*."

"Sweet," he murmured with a lingering caress, laughter riding his words, "help me here." With a gusty breath forced between his teeth, he moved her back a step. "I have a plan you're smashing to bits with your enthusiasm. As if I can ever forget you called it your treasure box."

He nudged her hand with his.

When she looked down, the velvet case was on his open palm.

"I'm sorry for everything," he said, tipping her chin until her gaze met his. His eyes were fathomless cerulean pools, devotion clear in their depths. "I wouldn't have let that horse's arse have you. Langston can't even hold a billiard stick properly, although he might be able to hang a bloody shelf. And I'm sorry I didn't show up at the chapel. I honestly didn't count on being tied to a chair in a rookery warehouse on the day of our wedding. But maybe—"

Halting the flow of words, she dusted her finger over his cheek. He reached, pressing the inside of her wrist to his lips, his breath scalding her skin. "I didn't love you then, Griffin Alastair Beckett, sixth Viscount Kent. Those vows would have been forced, whereas now, they won't be. You have my heart. You own every part of me. I'm sorry, too, for being tetchy. I didn't expect, that is, I didn't know lovemaking would be so...intimate. Even if one hears that it is, it's naught compared to the actual experience."

"It's actually fifth Viscount Kent, sweet, although it hardly matters." He took hold of her shoulder, his grip forceful. "You know it's never been that way for me, don't you? Not once, Willie, not *ever*. I was as astonished as you were, the feelings after. A tidal flood of them carrying me under." He shrugged, his smile the mischievous one she cherished. "I've never been in love, you see. Whole and utter love."

She turned the box around in a lazy circle in her hands. "That makes two of us."

"Don't forget this viscountess business, which is pointless, but there's no way around it. If you marry me, you're stuck, as I am. Officially a part of society, a trifling footnote in *Debrett's* our legacy. Are you sure your love can sustain that silliness?"

"I'm positively, without a doubt, undeniably certain that I love you, and my ardent feelings can sustain any and all titled ridiculousness." She actually believed she'd make a fine viscountess, whatever that involved.

At least there'd be no viscountess in England like her.

Cheeks flushing, Griff shifted from boot to boot, adorably anxious. "Go on, then, open it."

She tilted her head, recalling how horrid the last two weeks had been, with much of it his fault. He could wait a moment more. She gestured to the office. "Care to share your grand plan before I give my final answer?"

"My grand plan is to spend the rest of my life with you," he growled. "And you've already said yes and that you love me more than mathematics."

"Oh, you," she laughed and bounced on her toes to hug him. She stepped back when he tried to pull her in, dodging the hold. "I'm teasing you. You know I don't love anyone more than maths."

"You're enjoying this a little too much, Willie."

She lifted a brow, glancing about the office.

He exhaled softly, letting her go. Scrubbed his hand over the back of his neck, a sign of his exasperation. "I believe in you. If you want to rise above the crooked account books and manage investigations, I'll help you. I'll agree to this endeavor if you promise to travel with at least two footmen who can stomp a man into the ground and keep him there."

"You've already helped me," she reminded him, rubbing her thumb along the velvet box's rough nap. Tears were stinging her eyes, but she was determined not to cry, not yet. "Three jobs have come sliding in from the nobility this week. That's leagues above my regular clientele."

He shrugged, his gaze dancing away from her. *Oh,* his discomfort was endearing. "Like I said, I believe in you. It was nothing to mention at White's that I'd employed a discreet investigator for a matter of some delicacy. I'm stunned by how many queries I received, hence, printing the cards. This town is so pickled in problems you'll be in business for the next year from that one conversation alone. And we can't have these fancy fops traipsing to offices in Shoreditch, so I found you a better situation. What I could afford for now."

"This is perfect, Griff. It's simply perfect." She brushed a knuckle beneath each eye, her tears arriving along with a burst of tenderness for the man she loved. "The boy at the desk?"

He grinned, a weight seeming to lift from his shoulders. "Tobias Streeter. He's on loan from Jimmie Beans. Smart choice on my part, as the lad has more brains than anyone in that outfit."

Giggling, Mina gestured to the crooked shelf. "He's going to straighten your shelf."

"Figures himself an amateur architect if you can believe it, which of course, can never occur for someone born under such modest circumstance. I see something in him, so I'm going to provide more opportunities than he has in the slums."

"You take care of people," she whispered, swallowing hard. Griffin Beckett was good, kind, *true*. She'd not been mistaken.

He paused, considering, possibly willing to accept her judgment. "Streeter's honest and ambitious, not unlike the boy I once was, without an esteemed education and a fortunate birth. Being part Romani makes things difficult, even if his father is titled, which is all he'd tell me and likely all he ever will."

"I love you, Viscount Kent."

Reaching for her, he cradled her face, his fingers trembling against her cheek. "Marry me, Willie Wright."

"Yes," Mina said in a rush, "yes, yes, *yes*."

Griff took the box, flipped the top open and worked the ring free of its velvet folds. The fit was close to ideal, slipping only a little around her finger. The sapphire shone with glimmering hints of violet, a stone matching her eyes.

"I love it." She wiggled her fingers, turning her hand in the light. "Now that we've completed our business, are you ready to take me upstairs and show me that modest bedchamber? I have until two and my meeting with a dowager duchess."

Griff picked her up, nestling her against his chest. "Sweet, I thought you'd never ask."

EPILOGUE

Where a man counts his blessings and strives to hide his fears

A year later, in a small garden on a quiet lane
Marylebone, London

GRIFFIN BECKETT, VISCOUNT Kent, watched his wife dig in the microscopic patch of dirt behind her office, his heart tripping as it characteristically did when he was around her. Willie derived more pleasure from this sad little spot than she did the immense gardens at their Hertfordshire estate.

Whereas he derived pleasure from simply sitting in the sun with her. The trivial moments that made a *life*.

"Are you sure you're not too hot?" Griff shaded his eyes and glanced at the expanse of uncommonly blue sky. "It's rather warm today. Is your bonnet sturdy enough to protect you from the sun? It looks flimsy from here."

"Darling," she said, jamming her spade in the earth, "we talked about this. I'm fine. Healthy as a mule. I've agreed to an extra footman and a companion when I'm further along. More sleep, bigger breakfasts. Tobias is working another afternoon in addition to his standard two. You should see the terrace designs he showed me last week. They are extraordinary, if anyone will ever give him a chance."

Darling. It was a recent endearment, and Griff hadn't admitted this, but he adored it. "I'm searching for an apprenticeship position as he has no contacts, no education. He's talking about going into the Navy, which scares the blazes out of me. It's a tough sell locating a professional enterprise willing to employ a rookery lad, even if he's brilliant."

"You've been like a father to him."

"No, *no*. I don't know how to be a father," Griff repeated for at least the twentieth time, sipping from the single glass of brandy he allowed himself on summer afternoons. "The example provided me was indifferent at best and cruel at worst. What if I'm not good at it, Willie?"

Bracing her hand in the long stalks of grass, his wife glanced at him over her shoulder. Her abdomen was gently rounded, her breasts plump and crowding against the bodice of another of her unfortunate gowns. He couldn't think anything aside from: *she's bloody perfect. And she's mine.* "You're the kindest person I know, darling, with the most generous heart. You'll be a magnificent father in a town that doesn't know what that means. They attend yearly birthday parties and think they've done their jobs. Some hardly know their children's names."

"I'll be there every day, every hour." This was not a vow he took lightly. He wouldn't be like his father, not for one *second*. He loved his unborn child more than he'd believed possible already. How could he be anything less than present to cherish each moment?

As for his wife? There weren't words to describe his love for her. His happiness over the fulfilling life they were building together. Their incredible friendship, their undeniable passion.

He plucked a clover from the ground and twirled it between his fingers. "We can't break the bed again. I rolled on top of you last time, which might not be safe right now."

She choked on a laugh and continued burrowing in the dirt.

"And the cases you're handling. Nothing outside London until after the babe is born. Close to home and perhaps not the most interesting, if you take my meaning. Nothing stolen, nothing smuggled."

"I have a new assistant, as you know," she said and resumed planting the copse of begonias. She said nothing could kill them, not even her mishandling. "Miss Winifred will manage everything while I'm resting."

Griff skimmed the rim of his glass over his lips and ripped another clover free. "My business is keeping me at the warehouse until the wee hours some nights, then there's the work I'm doing at Wright's. I could arrange for sofas to be delivered to both offices for the nights you'd like to stay with me. Then we'll ride home together."

"A lumpy sofa in Limehouse? A sagging settee at Wright's Grand Derby? Where do I sign?" Shaking her head, she patted her spade on the mound of dirt. "Besides, I have the cats to take care of. We have four in the city now that we've brought two of your tiger oranges from the estate. I can't ask the staff to clean up cat droppings."

"Don't joke, Willie. I have five months to worry about you more than I already do."

She shoved to her feet, and he restrained himself from going to her because he knew she wouldn't like it. Crouching before his perch on the low brick wall bordering the property, she smiled gently. "I'm healthy, as is this baby." She took his hand and placed it on her belly. "Soon, we'll be able to feel him kick."

Griff's heart was what kicked. "Him?"

Willie lifted a slim shoulder in the most elegant of shrugs. "I have a feeling."

"I admire you, I do. You're so calm about this. While I'm"—he flexed his jaw, his breath shooting through his teeth—"nervous as hell. Up all night, staring at the ceiling kind of nerves."

His wife settled beside him, taking him into her arms. Comfort he willingly accepted, his brow finding the ideal spot in the crook of her neck. Her scent stole into his lungs, soothing him as it always did. "Because I'm certain. Sure. About you, about this family. I want as many children as we can create. How does five sound?"

"*Five*," he said, his voice cracking.

"Or just this one," she negotiated, sensing his panic. "One is perfect."

He nibbled on her jaw, pleased when she moaned lightly. "Two might be nice."

"Two would take more practice."

"Oh, sweet, you know how I *love* to practice."

"Arrange for the sofas, darling. Big, gorgeous ones I can sink into. I'll stay some nights not because I'm worried but to have more time together."

He lifted his head, his anguish easing. "I knew you'd see reason."

A flash of temper stole into her striking violet eyes. "Don't rejoice too early. I'm not going to follow every order, you know. Like a good little wife."

He tweaked her on the chin. "Viscountess Kent, don't I know it."

Easing to her feet, she tossed out her hand. "Come along. Mrs. Dove-Lyon will be here any moment for tea. She has a set of account ledgers she wants me to review."

Griff grumbled but did as he was told, linking his fingers with his wife's and rising to a stand. "She's more excited about this baby than I."

Willie sputtered out a laugh. "Hardly. There's not a man in England who's ever been this excited about a child."

A flush stole over his cheeks, leaving him unable to deny the statement. "I'm going to try to be wonderful, Wilhelmina Beckett. The best father in the history of fathers. The best husband."

"I'll hold you to that, darling." Willie laid her head against his arm as they strolled into the dwelling. "Every day for the rest of my life."

The End

Thank you for reading Griff and Willie's extraordinary love story! I'm thrilled to officially join the Lyon's Den family. This was such an incredible shared world to inhabit, and I enjoyed it immensely.

If you're interested in reading what happens to Tobias Streeter, Willie's erstwhile clerk and the resident hoodlum Griffin Beckett is trying to save, check out my novel, *The Brazen Bluestocking*. It's a few years later, and Tobias Streeter is now known as the Rogue King of Limehouse Basin. He's a rookery titan with a secret past who matches wits with a willful bluestocking (and a matchmaker of sorts) in a *steamy*, wild ride. It's also the first book in my popular, award-winning Duchess Society series.

I also put another fun nugget in *The Lyon Who Loved Me*. The time-piece Griff wears was created by none other than Christian Bainbridge, my hero in the Regency novella, *Tempting the Scoundrel*. ALL my heroes own a Bainbridge!

Please sign-up for my newsletter at tracy-sumner.com/newsletter to receive a free book (the award-winning steamy Regency novella, *Chasing the Duke*) and stay up-to-date about new releases, sales, contests and more. Amazon and Bookbub are good outlets for information, too! And, finally, I have a super fun reader's group, The Contrary Countesses, that can be found here: facebook.com/groups/tracysumner.

Happy reading, as always! Historical romance is the best.

xoxo
Tracy

To see a complete list of my books, visit me at:
www.tracy-sumner.com/books

About the Author

USA Today Bestselling author Tracy Sumner's storytelling career began when she picked up a historical romance on a college beach trip, and she fondly blames LaVyrle Spencer for her obsession with the genre. She's a recipient of the National Reader's Choice, HOLT Medallion, Golden Leaf, and Georgia Romance Writer's MAGGIE. When she's not writing sizzling love stories about feisty heroines and their temperamental-but-entirely-lovable heroes, Tracy enjoys reading, snowboarding, college football (Go Tigers!), yoga, and travel.